The Circus Boys Across The Continent

Edgar B. P. Darlington

Contents

THE CIRCUS BOYS ACROSS
THE CONTINENT

BY

Edgar B. P. Darlington

CHAPTER I
THE BOYS HEAR GOOD NEWS

Y ou never can guess it--you never can guess the news, Teddy," cried Phil Forrest, rushing into the gymnasium, his face flushed with excitement.

Teddy Tucker, clad in a pair of linen working trunks and a ragged, sleeveless shirt, both garments much the worse for their winter's wear, was lazily swinging a pair of Indian clubs.

"What is it, some kind of riddle, Phil?" he questioned, bringing the clubs down to his sides.

"Do be serious for a minute, won't you?"

"Me, serious? Why, I never cracked a smile. Isn't anything to smile at. Besides, do you know, since I've been in the circus business, every time I want to laugh I check myself so suddenly that it hurts?"

"How's that?"

"Because I think I've still got my makeup on and that I'll crack it if I laugh."

"What, your face?"

"My face? No! My makeup. By the time I remember that I haven't any makeup on I've usually forgotten what it was I wanted to laugh about. Then I don't laugh."

Teddy shied an Indian club at a rat that was scurrying across the far end of their gymnasium, missing him by half the width of the building.

"If you don't care, of course I shan't tell you. But it's good news, Teddy. You would say so if you knew it."

"What news? Haven't heard anything that sounds like news," his eyes fixed on the hole into which the rat had disappeared.

"You can't guess where we are going this summer?"

"Going? Don't have to guess. I know," answered the lad with an emphasizing nod.

"Where do you think?"

"We're going out with the Great Sparling Combined Shows, of course. Didn't we sign out for the season before we closed with the show last fall?"

"Yes, yes; but where?" urged Phil, showing him the letter he had just brought from the post office. "You couldn't guess if you tried."

"No. Never was a good guesser. That letter from Mr. Sparling?" he questioned, as his eyes caught the familiar red and gold heading used by the owner of the show.

"Yes."

"What's he want?"

"You know I wrote to him asking that we be allowed to skip the rehearsals before the show starts out, so that we could stay here and take our school examinations?"

Teddy nodded.

"I'd rather join the show," he grumbled.

"Never did see anything about school to go crazy over."

"You'll thank me someday for keeping you at it," said Phil. "See how well you have done this winter with your school work. I'm proud of you. Why, Teddy, there are lots of the boys a long way behind you. They can't say circus boys don't know anything just because they perform in a circus ring."

"H-m-m-m!" mused Teddy. "You haven't told me yet where we are going this summer. What's the route?"

"Mr. Sparling says that, as we are going to continue our last year's acts this season, there will be no necessity for rehearsals."

The announcement did not appear to have filled Teddy Tucker with joy.

"We do the flying rings again, then?"

"Yes. And we shall be able to give a performance that will surprise Mr. Sparling. Our winter's practicing has done a lot for us, as has our winter at school."

"Oh, I don't know."

"You probably will ride the educated mule again, while I expect to ride the elephant Emperor in the grand entry, as I did before. I'll be glad to get under the big top again, with the noise and the people, the music of the band and all that. Won't you, Teddy?" questioned Phil, his eyes glowing at the picture he had drawn.

Teddy heaved a deep sigh.

"Quit it!"

"Why?"

" 'Cause you make me think I'm there now."

Phil laughed softly.

"I can see myself riding the educated mule this very minute, kicking up the dust of the ring, making everybody get out of the way, and--"

"And falling off," laughed Phil. "You certainly are the most finished artist in the show when it comes to getting into trouble."

"Yes; I seem to keep things going," grinned the lad.

"But I haven't told you all that Mr. Sparling says in the letter."

"What else does he say?"

"That the show is to start from its winter quarters, just outside of Germantown, Pennsylvania, on April twenty-second--"

"Let's see; just two weeks from today," nodded Teddy.

"Yes."

"I wish it was today."

"He says we are to report on the twenty-first, as the show leaves early in the evening."

"Where do we show first?"

"Atlantic City. Then we take in the Jersey Coast towns--"

"Do we go to New York?"

"New York? Oh, no! The show isn't big enough for New York quite yet, even if it is a railroad show now. We've got to grow some before that. Mighty few shows are large enough to warrant taking them into the big city."

"How do you know?"

"All the show people say that."

"Pshaw! I'd sure make a hit in New York with the mule."

"Time enough for that later. You and I will yet perform in Madison Square Garden. Just put that down on your route card, Teddy Tucker."

"Humph! If we don't break our necks before that! Where did you say we were--"

"After leaving New Jersey, we are to play through New York State, taking in the big as well as the small towns, and from Buffalo heading straight west. Mr. Sparling writes that we are going across the continent."

"What?"

"Says he's going to make the Sparling Shows known from the Atlantic to the Pacific--"

"Across the continent!" exclaimed Teddy unbelievingly. "No; you're fooling."

"Yes; clear to the Pacific Coast. We're going to San Francisco, too. What do you think of that, Teddy?"

"Great! Wow! Whoop!" howled the boy, hurling his remaining Indian Club far up among the rafters of the gymnasium, whence it came clattering down, both lads laughing gleefully.

"We're going to see the country this time, and we shan't have to sleep out in an open canvas wagon, either."

"Where shall we sleep?"

"Probably in a car."

"It won't be half so much fun," objected Teddy.

"I imagine the life will be different. Perhaps we shall not have so much fun, but we'll have the satisfaction of knowing that we are part of a real show. It will mean a lot to us to be with an organization like that. It will give us a better standing in the profession, and possibly by another season we may be able to get with one of the really big ones. Next spring, if we have good luck, we shall have finished with our school here. If they'll have us, we'll try to join out with one of them. In the meantime we must work hard, Teddy, so we shall be in fine shape when we join out two weeks from today. Come on; I'll wrestle you a few falls."

"Done," exclaimed Teddy.

Phil promptly threw off his coat and vest. A few minutes later the lads were struggling on the wrestling mat, their faces dripping with perspiration, their supple young figures twisting and turning as each struggled for the mastery of the other.

The readers of the preceding volume in this series, entitled, THE CIRCUS BOYS ON THE FLYING RINGS, will recognize Phil and Teddy at once as the lads who had so unexpectedly joined the Sparling Combined Shows the previous summer. It was Phil who, by his ready resourcefulness, saved the life of the wife of the owner of the show as well as that of an animal trainer later on. Then, too, it will be remembered how the lad became the fast friend of the great elephant Emperor, which he rescued from "jail," and with which he performed in the ring to the delight of thousands. Ere the close of the season both boys had won their way to the flying rings, thus becoming full-fledged circus performers. Before leaving the show they had signed out for another season at a liberal salary.

With their savings, which amounted to a few hundred dollars, the boys had returned to their home at Edmeston, there to put in the winter at school.

That they might lose nothing of their fine physical condition, the Circus Boys had rented an old carpenter shop, which they rigged up as a gymnasium, fitting it with flying rings, trapeze bars and such other equipment as would serve to keep them in trim for the coming season's work.

Here Phil and Teddy had worked long hours after school. During the winter they had gained marked improvement in their work, besides developing some entirely new acts on the flying rings. During this time they had been living with Mrs. Cahill, who, it will be remembered, had proved herself a real friend to the motherless boys.

Now, the long-looked-for day was almost at hand when they should once more join the canvas city for a life in the open.

The next two weeks were busy ones for the lads, with their practice and the hard study incident to approaching examinations. Both boys passed with high standing. Books were put away, gymnasium apparatus stored and one sunlit morning two slender, manly looking young fellows, their faces reflecting perfect health and happiness, were at the railroad station waiting for the train which should bear them to the winter quarters of the show.

Fully half the town had gathered to see them off, for Edmeston was justly proud of its Circus Boys. As the train finally drew up and the lads clambered aboard, their school companions set up a mighty shout, with three cheers for the Circus Boys.

"Don't stick your head in the lion's mouth, Teddy!" was the parting salute Phil and Teddy received from the boys as the train drew out.

"Well, Teddy, we're headed for the Golden Gate at last!" glowed Phil.

"You bet!" agreed Teddy with more force than elegance.

"I wonder if old Emperor will remember me, Teddy?"

"Sure thing! But, do you think that 'fool mule,' as Mr. Sparling calls him, will remember me? Or will he want to kick me full of holes before the season has really opened?"

"I shouldn't place too much dependence on a mule," laughed Phil. "Come on; let's go inside and sit down."

CHAPTER II
ON THE ROAD ONCE MORE

All was bustle and excitement.

Men were rushing here and there, shouting out hoarse commands. Elephants were trumpeting shrilly, horses neighing; while, from many a canvas-wrapped wagon savage beasts of the jungle were emitting roar upon roar, all voicing their angry protest at being removed from the winter quarters where they had been at rest for the past six months.

The Great Sparling Combined Shows were moving out for their long summer's journey. The long trains were being rapidly loaded when Phil Forrest and Teddy Tucker arrived on the scene late in the afternoon.

It was all new and strange to them, unused as they were to the ways of a railroad show. Their baggage had been sent on ahead of them, so they did not have that to bother with. Each carried a suitcase, however, and the boys were now trying to find someone in authority to ask where they should go and what they should do.

"Hello, Phil, old boy!" howled a familiar voice.

"Who's that?" demanded Teddy.

"Why, it's Rod Palmer, our working mate on the rings!" cried Phil, dropping his bag and darting across the tracks, where he had espied a shock of very red hair that he knew could belong only to Rodney Palmer.

Teddy strolled over with rather more dignity.

"Howdy?" he greeted just as Phil and the red-haired boy were wringing each other's hands. "Anybody'd think you two were long lost brothers."

"We are, aren't we, Rod?" glowed Phil.

"And we have been, ever since you boys showed me the brook where I could wash my face back in that tank town where you two lived. That was last summer.

Seems like it was yesterday."

"Yes, and we work together again, I hear? I'm glad of that. I guess you've been doing something this winter," decided Rodney, after a critical survey of the lads. "You sure are both in fine condition. Quite a little lighter than you were last season, aren't you, Phil?"

"No; I weigh ten pounds more."

"Then you must be mighty hard."

"Hard as a keg of nails, but I hope not quite so stiff," laughed Phil.

"What you been working at?"

"Rings, mostly. We've done some practicing on the trapeze. What did you do all winter?"

"Me? Oh, I joined a team that was playing vaudeville houses. I was the second man in a ring act. Made good money and saved most of it. Why didn't you join out for the vaudeville?"

"We spent our winter at school," answered Phil.

"That's a good stunt at that. In the tank town, I suppose?" grinned the red-haired boy.

"You might call it that, but it's a pretty good town, just the same," replied Phil. "I saw many worse ones while we were out last season."

"And you'll see a lot more this season. Wait till we get to playing some of those way-back western towns. I was out there with a show once, and I know what I'm talking about. Where are you berthed?"

"I don't know," answered Phil. "Where are you?"

"Car number fourteen. Haven't seen the old man, then?"

"Mr. Sparling? No. And I want to see him at once. Where shall I find him?"

"He was here half an hour ago. Maybe he's in his office."

"Where is that?"

"Private car number one. Yes; the old man has his own elegant car this season. He's living high, I tell you. No more sleeping out in an old wagon that has no springs. It will be great to get into a real bed every night, won't it?"

Teddy shook his head doubtfully.

"I don't know 'bout that."

"I should think it would be pretty warm on a hot night," nodded Phil.

"And what about the rainy nights?" laughed Rodney. "Taking it altogether, I guess I'll take the Pullman for mine--"

"There goes Mr. Sparling now," interjected Teddy.

"Where?"

"Just climbing aboard a car. See him?"

"That's number one," advised Rodney. "Better skip, if you want to catch him. He's hard to land today. There's a lot for him to look after."

"Yes; come on, Teddy. Get your grip," said Phil, hurrying over to where he had dropped his suitcase.

"But it's going to be a great show," called Rodney.

"Especially the flying-ring act," laughed Phil.

A few minutes later both boys climbed aboard the private car, and, leaving their bags on the platform, pushed open the door and entered.

Mr. Sparling was seated at a roll-top desk in an office-like compartment, frowning over some document that he held in his hand.

The boys waited until he should look up. He did so suddenly, peering at them from beneath his heavy eyebrows. Phil was not sure, from the showman's expression, whether he had recognized them or not. Mr. Sparling answered this question almost at once.

"How are you, Forrest? Well, Tucker, I suppose you've come back primed to put my whole show to the bad, eh?"

"Maybe," answered Teddy carelessly.

"Oh, maybe, eh? So that's the way the flag's blowing, is it? Well, you let me catch you doing it and--stand up here, you two, and let me look at you."

He gazed long and searchingly at the Circus Boys, noting every line of their slender, shapely figures.

"You'll do," he growled.

"Yes, sir," answered Phil, smiling.

"Shake hands."

Mr. Sparling thrust out both hands toward them with almost disconcerting suddenness.

"Ouch!" howled Teddy, writhing under the grip the showman gave him, but if Phil got a pressure of equal force he made no sign.

"Where's your baggage?"

"We sent our trunks on yesterday. I presume they are here somewhere, sir."

"If they're not in your car, let me know."

"If you will be good enough to tell me where our car is I will find out at once."

The showman consulted a typewritten list.

"You are both in car number eleven. The porter will show you the berths that have been assigned to you, and I hope you will both obey the rules of the cars."

"Oh, yes, sir," answered Phil.

"I know you will, but I'm not so sure of your fat friend here. I think it might be a good plan to tie him in his berth, or he'll be falling off the platform some night, get under the wheels and wreck the train."

"I don't walk in my sleep," answered Teddy.

"Oh, you don't?"

"I don't."

Mr. Sparling frowned; then his face broke out into a broad smile.

"I always said you were hopeless. Run along, and get settled now. You understand that you will keep your berth all season, don't you?"

"Yes, sir. What time do we go out?"

"One section has already gone. The next and last will leave tonight about ten o'clock. We want to make an early start, for the labor is all green. It'll take three times as long to put up the rag as usual."

"The rag? What's the rag?" questioned Teddy.

"Beg pardon," mocked Mr. Sparling. "I had forgotten that you are still a Reuben. A rag is a tent, in show parlance."

"Oh!"

"Any orders after we get settled?" asked Phil.

"Nothing for you to do till parade time tomorrow. You will look to the same executives that you did last year. There has been no change in them."

The lads hurried from the private car, and after searching about the railroad yard for fully half an hour they came upon car number eleven. This was a bright, orange-colored car with the name of the Sparling Shows painted in gilt letters near the roof, just under the eaves. The smell of fresh paint was everywhere, but the wagons being covered with canvas made it impossible for them to see how the new wagons looked. There were many of these loaded on flat cars, with which the rail-road yard seemed to be filled.

"Looks bigger than Barnum & Bailey's," nodded Teddy, feeling a growing pride that he was connected with so great an organization.

"Not quite, I guess," replied Phil, mounting the platform of number eleven.

The boys introduced themselves to the porter, who showed them to their berths. These were much like those in the ordinary sleeper, except that the up-per berths had narrow windows looking out from them. Across each berth was stretched a strong piece of twine.

Phil asked the porter what the string was for.

"To hang your trousers on, sah," was the enlightening answer. "There's hooks for the rest of your clothes just outside the berths."

"This looks pretty good to me," said Phil, peering out through the screened window of his berth.

"Reminds me of when I used to go to sleep in the woodbox behind the stove where I lived last year in Edmeston," grumbled Teddy in a muffled voice, as he rummaged about his berth trying to accustom himself to it. Teddy never had ridden in a sleeping car, so it was all new and strange to him.

"Say, who sleeps upstairs?" he called to the porter.

"The performers, sah--some of them. This heah is the performers' car, sah."

"How do they get up there? On a rope ladder?"

Phil shouted.

"You ninny, this isn't a circus performance. No; of course they don't climb up on a rope ladder as if they were starting a trapeze act."

"How, then?"

"The porter brings out a little step ladder, and it's just like walking upstairs, only it isn't."

"Huh!" grunted Teddy. "Do they have a net under them all night?"

"A net? What for?"

"Case they fall out of bed."

"Put him out!" shouted several performers who were engaged in settling them-selves in their own quarters. "He's too new for this outfit."

Phil drew his companion aside and read him a lecture on not asking so many questions, advising Teddy to keep his ears and eyes open instead.

Teddy grumbled and returned to the work of unpacking his bag.

Inquiry for their trunks developed the fact that they would have to look for these in the baggage car; that no trunks were allowed in the sleepers.

Everything about the car was new and fresh, the linen white and clean, while the wash room, with its mahogany trimmings, plate glass mirrors and upholstered seats, was quite the most elaborate thing that Teddy had ever seen.

He called to Phil to come and look at it.

"Yes, it is very handsome. I am sure we shall get to be very fond of our home on wheels before the season is ended. I'm going out now to see if our trunks have arrived."

Phil, after some hunting about, succeeded in finding the baggage man of the train, from whom he learned that the trunks had arrived and were packed away in the baggage car.

By this time night had fallen. With it came even greater confusion, while torches flared up here and there to light the scene of bustle and excitement.

It was all very confusing to Phil, and he was in constant fear of being run down by switching engines that were shunting cars back and forth as fast as they were loaded, rapidly making up the circus train. The Circus Boy wondered if he ever could get used to being with a railroad show.

"I must be getting back or I shall not be able to find number eleven," decided Phil finally. "I really haven't the least idea where it is now."

The huge canvas-covered wagons stood up in the air like a procession of wraiths of the night, muttered growls and guttural coughs issuing from their interiors. All this was disturbing to one not used to it.

Phil started on a run across the tracks in search of his car.

In the meantime Teddy Tucker, finding himself alone, had sauntered forth to watch the loading, and when he ventured abroad trouble usually followed.

The lad soon became so interested in the progress of the work that he was excitedly shouting out orders to the men, offering suggestions and criticisms of the way they were doing that work.

Now, most of the men in the labor gang were new--that is, they had not been with the Sparling show the previous season, and hence did not know Teddy by sight. After a time they tired of his running fire of comment. They had several times roughly warned him to go on about his business. But Teddy did not heed their advice, and likewise forgot all about that which Phil had given him earlier in the evening.

He kept right on telling the men how to load the circus, for, if there was one thing in the world that Teddy Tucker loved more than another it was to "boss" somebody.

All at once the lad felt himself suddenly seized from behind and lifted off his feet. At the same time a rough hand was clapped over his mouth.

The Circus Boy tried to utter a yell, but he found it impossible for him to do so. Teddy kicked and fought so vigorously that it was all his captor could do to hold him.

"Come and help me. We'll fix the fresh kid this time," called the fellow in whose grip the lad was struggling.

"What's the matter, Larry? Is he too much for you?" laughed the other man.

"He's the biggest little man I ever got my fists on. Gimme a hand here."

"What are you going to do with him?"

"I'll show you in a minute."

"Maybe he's with the show. He's slippery enough to be a performer."

"No such thing. And I don't care if he is. I'll teach him not to interfere with the men. Grab hold and help me carry him."

Together they lifted the kicking, squirming, fighting boy, carrying him on down the tracks, not putting him down until they had reached the standpipe of a nearby water tank, where the locomotives took on their supply of fresh water.

"Jerk that spout around!" commanded Larry, sitting down on Tucker with a force that made the lad gasp.

"Can't reach the chain."

"Then get a pike pole, and be quick about it. The foreman will be looking for us first thing we know. If he finds us here he'll fire us before we get started."

"See here, Larry, what are you going to do?" demanded the other suspiciously.

"My eyes, but you're inquisitive! Going to wash the kid down. Next time mebby he won't be so fresh."

And "wash" they did.

Suddenly the full stream from the standpipe spurted down. Larry promptly let go of his captive. Teddy was right in the path of the downpour, and the next instant he was struggling in the flood.

The showman dropped him and started to run.

Teddy let out a choking howl, grasping frantically for his tormentor. A moment later the lad's hands closed over Larry's ankles, and before the man was able to free himself from the boy's grip Teddy had pulled him down and dragged him under the stream that was pouring down in a perfect deluge. The Circus Boy, being strong and muscular, was able to accomplish this with slight exertion.

Larry's companion was making no effort to assist his fallen comrade. Instead, the fellow was howling with delight.

No sooner, however, had Teddy raised the man and slammed him down on his back under the spout, than the lad let go of his victim and darted off into the shadows. Teddy realized that it was high time he was leaving.

The man, fuming with rage, uttering loud-voiced threats of vengeance, scrambled out of the flood and began rushing up and down the tracks in search of Teddy.

But the boy was nowhere to be found. He had hastily climbed over a fence, where he crouched, dripping wet, watching the antics of the enraged Larry.

"Guess he won't bother another boy right away," grinned Teddy, not heeding his own wet and bedraggled condition.

The two showmen finally gave up their quest, and all at once started on a run in the opposite direction.

"Now, I wonder what's made them run away like that? Surely they aren't scared of me. I wonder? Guess I'll go over and find out."

Leaving his hiding place, the lad retraced his steps across the tracks until finally, coming up with a man, who proved to be the superintendent of the yard, Teddy asked him where sleeping car number eleven was located.

"Eleven? The sleepers have all gone, young man."

"G-g-gone?"

"Yes."

"But I thought--"

"Went out regular on the 9:30 express."

Teddy groaned. Here he was, left behind before the show had all gotten away from its winter quarters. But he noted that the train bearing the cages and other equipment was still in the yard. There was yet a chance for him.

"Wha--what time does that train go?" he asked pointing to the last section.

"Going now. Why, what's the matter with you youngster? The train is moving now."

"Going? The matter is that I've got to go with them," cried the lad, suddenly darting toward the moving train.

"Come back here! Come back! Do you want to be killed?"

"I've got to get on that train!" Teddy shouted back at the superintendent.

The great stock cars were rumbling by as the boy drew near the track, going faster every moment. By the light of a switch lamp Teddy could make out a ladder running up to the roof of one of the box cars.

He could hear the yard superintendent running toward him shouting.

"He'll have me, if I don't do something. Then I will be wholly left," decided Teddy. "I'm going to try it."

As the big stock car slipped past him the lad sprang up into the air, his eyes fixed on the ladder. His circus training came in handy here, for Teddy hit the mark unerringly, though it had been considerably above his head. The next second his fingers closed over a rung of the ladder, and there he hung, dangling in the air, with the train now rushing over switches, rapidly gaining momentum as it stretched out headed for the open country.

CHAPTER III
PHIL TO RESCUE

Phil Forrest was in a panic of uneasiness.

No sooner had his own section started than he made the discovery that Teddy Tucker was not on board. Then the lad went through the train in the hope that his companion had gotten on the wrong car. There was no trace of Teddy.

In the meantime Teddy had slowly clambered to the roof of the stock car, where he stretched himself out, clinging to the running board, with the big car swaying beneath him. The wind seemed, up there, to be blowing a perfect gale, and it was all the boy could do to hold on. After a while he saw a light approaching him. The light was in the hands of a brakeman who was working his way over the train toward the caboose.

He soon came up to where Teddy was lying. There he stopped.

"Well, youngster, what are you doing here?" he demanded, flashing his light into the face of the uncomfortable Teddy.

"Trying to ride."

"I suppose you know you are breaking the law and that I'll have to turn you over to a policeman or a constable the next town we stop at?"

"Nothing of the sort! What do you take me for? Think I'm some kind of tramp?" objected the lad. "Go on and let me alone."

The brakeman looked closer. He observed that the boy was soaking wet, but that, despite this, he was well dressed.

"What are you, if not a tramp?"

"I'm with the show."

The brakeman laughed long and loud, but Teddy was more interested in the man's easy poise on the swaying car than in what he said.

"Wish I could do that," muttered the lad admiringly.

"What's that?"

"Nothing, only I was thinking out loud."

"Well, you'll get off at the next stop unless you can prove that you belong here."

"I won't," protested Teddy stubbornly.

"We'll see about that. Come down here on the flat car behind this one, and we'll find out. I see some of the show people there. Besides, you're liable to fall off here and get killed. Come along."

"I can't."

"Why not?"

"I'll fall off if I try to get up."

"And you a showman?" laughed the brakeman satirically, at the same time grabbing Teddy by the coat collar and jerking him to his feet.

The trainman did not appear to mind the giddy swaying of the stock car. He permitted Teddy to walk on the running board while he himself stepped carelessly along on the sloping roof of the car, though not relaxing his grip on the collar of Teddy Tucker.

Bidding the boy to hang to the brake wheel, the brakeman began climbing down the end ladder, so as to catch Teddy in case he were to fall. After him came the Circus Boy, cautiously picking his way down the ladder.

"Any of you fellows know this kid?" demanded the trainman, flashing his lantern into Teddy's face. "He says he's with the show."

"Put him off!" howled one of the roustabouts who had been sleeping on the flat car under a cage. "Never saw him before."

"You sit down there, young man. Next stop, off you go," announced the brakeman sternly.

"I'll bet you I don't," retorted Teddy Tucker aggressively.

"We'll see about that."

"Quit your music; we want to go to sleep," growled a showman surlily.

The brakeman put down his lantern and seated himself on the side of the flat car. He did not propose to leave the boy until he had seen him safely off the train.

"How'd you get wet?" questioned Tucker's captor.

"Some fellows ducked me."

The trainman roared, which once more aroused the ire of the roustabouts who were trying to sleep.

They had gone on for an hour, when finally the train slowed down.

"Here's where you hit the ties," advised the brakeman, peering ahead.

"Where are we?"

"McQueen's siding. We stop here to let an express by. And I want to tell you that it won't be healthy for you if I catch you on this train again. Now, get off!"

Teddy making no move to obey, the railroad man gently but firmly assisted him over the side of the car, dropping him down the embankment by the side of the track.

"I'll make you pay for this if I ever catch you again," threatened Teddy from the bottom of the bank, as he scrambled to his feet.

Observing that the trainman was holding his light over the side of the car and peering down at him, Teddy ran along on all fours until he was out of sight of the brakeman, then he straightened up and ran toward the rear of the train as fast as his feet would carry him, while the railroad man began climbing over the cars again, headed for the caboose at the rear.

Teddy had gained the rear of the train by this time, but he did not show himself just yet. He waited until the flagman had come in, and until the fellow who had put him off had disappeared in the caboose.

At that, Teddy sprang up, and, swinging to the platform of the caboose, quickly climbed the iron ladder that led to the roof of the little boxlike car. He had no sooner flattened himself on the roof than the train began to move again.

Only one more stop was made during the night and that for water. Just before daylight they rumbled into the yards at Atlantic City, and Teddy scrambled from his unsteady perch, quickly clambering down so as to be out of the way before the trainmen should discover his presence.

But quickly as he had acted, he had not been quick enough. The trainman who had put him off down the line collared the lad the minute his feet touched the platform of the caboose.

"You here again?" he demanded sternly.

Teddy grinned sheepishly.

"I told you you couldn't put me off."

"We'll see about that. Here, officer." He beckoned to a policeman. "This kid has been stealing a ride. I put him off once. I turn him over to you now."

"All right. Young man, you come with me!"

Teddy protested indignantly, but the officer, with a firm grip on his arm, dragged the lad along with him. They proceeded on up the tracks toward the station, the lad insisting that he was with the show and that he had a right to ride wherever he pleased.

"Teddy!" shouted a voice, just as they stepped on the long platform that led down to the street.

"Phil!" howled the lad. "Come and save me! A policeman's got me and he's taking me to jail."

Phil Forrest ran to them.

"Here, here! What's this boy done?" he demanded.

CHAPTER IV
RENEWING OLD ACQUAINTANCES

W ell, Teddy, I must say you have made a good start," grinned Phil, after necessary explanations had been made and the young Circus Boy had been released by the policeman who had him in tow." A few minutes more and you would have been in a police station. I can imagine how pleased Mr. Sparling would have been to hear that."

Teddy hung his head.

"Your clothes are a sight, too. How did--what happened? Did you fall in a creek, or something of that sort?"

The lad explained briefly how he had been captured by the two men and ducked under the standpipe of the water tank.

"But I soaked him, too," Tucker added triumphantly." And I'm going to soak him again. The first man I come across whose name is Larry is going to get it from me," threatened the lad, shaking his fist angrily.

"You come over to the sleeper with me and get into some decent looking clothes. I'm ashamed of you, Teddy Tucker."

"So am I," grinned the boy as they turned to go, Phil leading the way to the car number eleven, from which the performers were beginning to straggle, rubbing their eyes and stretching themselves.

The change of clothing having been made, the lads started for the lot, hoping that they might find the old coffee stand and have a cup before breakfast. To their surprise, upon arriving at the lot, they found the cook tent up and the breakfast cooking.

"Why, how did you ever get this tent here and up so quickly?" asked Phil after they had greeted their old friend of the cook tent.

"Came in on the flying squadron. This is a railroad show now, you know," answered the head steward, after greeting the boys.

"Flying squadron? What's that?" demanded Teddy, interested at once.

"The flying squadron is the train that goes out first. It carries the cook tent and other things that will be needed first. We didn't have that last year. You'll find a lot of new things, and some that you won't like as well as you did when we had the old road show. What's your act this year?"

"Same as last."

"Elephant?"

"Yes, and the rings. My friend Teddy I expect will ride the educated mule again."

While they were talking the steward was preparing a pot of steaming coffee for them, which he soon handed over to the lads with a plate of wafers, of which they disposed in short order.

It was broad daylight by this time, and the boys decided to go out and watch the erection of the tents. It was all new and full of interest to them. As they caught the odor of trampled grass and the smell of the canvas their old enthusiasm came back to them with added force.

"It's great to be a circus man, isn't it, Phil?" breathed Teddy.

"It is unless one is getting into trouble all the time, the way you do. I expect that, some of these days, you'll get something you don't want."

"What?"

"Oh, I don't know. But I am sure it will be something quite serious."

"You better look out for yourself," growled Teddy. "I'll take care of myself."

"Yes; the way you did last night," retorted Phil, with a hearty laugh. "Come on, now; let's not quarrel. I want to find some of our old friends. Isn't that Mr. Miaco over there by the dressing tent?"

"Sure."

Both lads ran toward their old friend, the head clown, with outstretched hands, and Mr. Miaco, seeing them coming, hastened forward to greet them.

"Well, well, boys! How are you?"

"Oh, we're fine," glowed Phil. "And we are glad to be back again, let me tell you."

"No more so than your old friends are to have you back. Same old act?"

"Yes."

"What have you boys been doing this winter?"

"Studying and exercising."

"Yes; I knew, from your condition, that you have been keeping up your work. Got anything new?"

"Not much. Trapeze."

"Good! I'll bet you will be in some of the flying-bar acts before the season is over. We have a lot of swell performers this season."

"So I have heard. Who are some of them?"

"Well, there's the Flying Four."

"Who are they?" questioned Teddy.

"Trapeze performers. They're great--the best in the business. And then there's The Limit."

"Talk United States," demanded Teddy. "The Limit? Whoever heard of that?"

"In other words, the Dip of Death."

Teddy shook his head helplessly.

"That is the somersaulting automobile. A pretty young woman rides in it, and some fine day she won't. I never did like those freak acts. But the public does," sighed the old circus man. "The really difficult feats, that require years of practice, patrons don't seem to give a rap for. But let somebody do a stunt in which he is in danger of suddenly ending his life, then you'll see the people howl with delight. I sometimes think they would be half tickled to death to see some of us break our necks. There's a friend of yours, Phil."

"Who?"

"Emperor, the old elephant that you rode last year. They are taking him to the menagerie tent."

"Whistle to him, Phil," suggested Teddy.

Phil uttered a low, peculiar whistle.

The big elephant's ears flapped. The procession that he was leading came to a sudden stop and Emperor trumpeted shrilly.

"He hasn't forgotten me," breathed Phil happily. "Dear old Emperor!"

"Pipe him up again," urged Teddy.

"No; I wouldn't dare. He would be likely to break away from Mr. Kennedy and might trample some of the people about here. See, Mr. Kennedy is having his troubles as it is."

"Done any tumbling since you closed last fall?" questioned Mr. Miaco.

"We have practiced a little. I want to learn, if you will teach me--"

"Why, you can tumble already, Phil."

"Yes; but I want to do something better--the springboard."

"They've got a leaping act this year."

"How?"

"Performers and clowns leap over a herd of elephants. You've seen the act, haven't you?"

"Oh, yes; I know what it is. I wish I were able to do it."

"You will be. It is not difficult, only one has to have a natural bent for it. Now, your friend Teddy ought to make a fine leaper."

"I am," interposed Teddy pompously. "I always was."

"Yes; you're the whole show from your way of thinking," laughed Mr. Miaco. "I must go see if my trunk is placed. See you later, boys."

After leaving the clown, the lads strolled about the lot. They soon discovered that the Sparling Shows was a big organization. The tents had been very much enlarged and the canvas looked new and white.

In the menagerie tent the boys found many new cages, gorgeous in red and gold, with a great variety of animals that had not been in the show the previous summer.

Emperor's delight at seeing his little friend again was expressed in loud trumpetings, and his sinuous trunk quickly found its way into Phil Forrest's pocket in search of sweets. And Emperor was not disappointed. In one coat pocket he found a liberal supply of candy, while the other held a bag of peanuts, to all of which the big elephant helped himself freely until no more was left.

"Have you got my trappings ready, Mr. Kennedy?" asked Phil of the keeper.

"You'll find the stuff in fine shape. The old man has had a new bonnet made for Emperor and a new blanket. He'll be right smart when he enters the ring today. Been over to the cook tent yet?"

"Yes; but not for breakfast. We are going soon now. We want to see them raise the big top first."

When the boys had passed out into the open they observed the big circus tent rising slowly from the ground where it had been laid out, the various pieces laced together by nimble fingers. Mr. Sparling was on the lot watching everything at the same time. This was the first time the tent had been pitched, and, as has been said before, most of the men were green at their work. Yet, under the boisterous prodding of the boss canvasman, the white city was going up rapidly and with some semblance of system.

As soon as the dome of the big top left the ground the boys crawled under and went inside. Here all was excitement and confusion. Men were shouting their commands, above which the voice of the boss canvasman rose distinctly.

The dome of the tent by this time was halfway up the long, green center pole, while men were hurrying in with quarter poles on their shoulders, and which they quickly stood on end and guided into place in the bellying canvas.

The eyes of the Circus Boys sparkled with enthusiasm.

"I wish we were up there on the rings," breathed Teddy.

"We shall be soon, old fellow," answered Phil, patting him on the shoulder. "And for many days after this, I hope. Hello, I wonder what's wrong up there?"

Phil's quick glance had caught something up near the half-raised dome that impressed him as not being right.

"Look out aloft!" he sang out warningly.

"The key rope's going. Grab the other line!" bellowed the boss canvasman.

"You fools!" roared Mr. Sparling from the opposite side of the tent, as he quickly noted what was happening. "Run for your lives! You'll have the whole outfit down on your heads!"

The men fled, letting go of ropes and poles, diving for places of safety, many of them knowing what it meant to have that big tent collapse and descend upon them.

The man who had held the key rope was the one who had been at fault. Some of the new men had called to him to give them a hand on another line, and he, a new man himself, all forgetful of the important task that had been assigned to him, dropped the key rope, as it is called, turning to assist his associate.

Instantly the dome of the big top began to settle with a grating noise as the huge iron ring in the peak began slipping down the center pole.

The key rope coiled on the ground was running out and squirming up into the air. Only a single coil of it remained when Phil suddenly darted forward. With a bound, he threw himself upon the rope, giving it a quick twist about his arm.

The instant Phil had fastened his grip upon the rope he shot up into the air so quickly that the onlookers failed to catch the meaning of his sudden flight.

One pair of eyes, however, saw and understood. They belonged to Mr. Sparling, the owner of the show.

"The boy will he killed!" he groaned. "Let go!"

CHAPTER V
DOING A MAN'S WORK

For one brief instant Phil Forrest's head was giddy and his breath fairly left his body from the speed with which he was propelled upward on the key rope.

But the lad had not for a second lost his presence of mind. Below him was some eight feet of the rope dangling in the air.

With a sudden movement that could only have been executed by one with unusual strength and agility, Phil let the rope slip through his hands just enough to slacken his speed. Instantly he threw himself around the center pole, twisting the rope around and around it, each twist slackening his upward flight a little. He knew that, were his head to strike the iron ring in the dome at the speed he was traveling, he would undoubtedly be killed. It was as much to prevent this as to save the tent that Phil took the action he did, though his one real thought was to save his employer's property.

Now the rapid upward shoot had dwindled to a slow, gradual slipping of the rope as it moved up the center pole inch by inch. But Phil's peril was even greater than before. The moment that heavy iron ring began pressing down on his head and shoulders with the weight of the canvas behind it, there would be nothing for him to do but to let go.

A forty-foot fall to the hard ground below seemed inevitable. Yet he did not lose his presence of mind for an instant.

"Give him a hand!" yelled the boss canvasman.

"How? How?" shouted the canvasmen. "We can't reach him."

"Get a net under that boy, you blockheads!" thundered Mr. Sparling, rushing over from his station. "Don't you see he's bound to fall, and if he does he'll break

his neck?"

The boss canvasman ordered three of his men to get the trapeze performers' big net that lay in a heap near the ring nearest the dressing tent, for there were two rings now in the Great Sparling Combined Shows.

They dragged it over as quickly as possible; then willing hands grabbed it and stretched the heavy net out. At Mr. Sparling's direction the four corners of the net were manned and the safety device raised from the ground, ready to catch the lad should he fall.

"Now let go and drop!" roared Mr. Sparling.

They heard Phil laugh from his lofty perch.

"Jump, I say!"

"What, and let the tent down on you all?"

By this time the lad had curled his feet up over his head, and they saw that he was bracing his feet against the iron ring, literally holding the tent up with his own powerful muscles. Of course, as a matter of fact, Phil was holding a very small part of the weight of the tent, but as it was, the strain was terrific.

Hanging head down, his face flushed until it seemed as if the blood must burst through the skin, he hung there as calmly as if he were not in imminent peril of his life. Then, too, there was the danger to those below him. If the tent should collapse some of them would be killed, for there were now few quarter poles in place to break the fall of the heavy canvas.

"I say, down there!" he cried, finally managing to make himself heard above the uproar.

"Are you going to drop?" shouted Mr. Sparling.

"No; do you want me to let the tent drop on you? If you'll all get out there'll be fewer hurt in case I have to let go."

"That boy!" groaned the showman.

"Toss me a line and be quick about it," called Phil shrilly.

"What can you do with a line?" demanded the showman, now more excited than he had ever been in his life.

"Toss it!"

"Give him a line!"

"A strong one," warned Phil, his voice not nearly as far reaching as it had been.

"A line!" bellowed Mr. Sparling. "He knows what he wants it for, and he's got more sense than the whole bunch of us."

A coil of rope shot up. But it missed Phil by about six feet.

Another one was forthcoming almost instantly. This time, however, Mr. Sparling snatched it from the hands of the showman who had made the wild cast.

"Idiot!" he roared, pushing the man aside.

Once more the coil sailed up, unrolling as it went. This time Phil grasped it with his free hand, which he had liberated for the purpose.

"Now, be careful," warned Mr. Sparling. "I don't know what you think you're going to do; but whatever you start you're sure to finish."

To this Phil made no reply. He was getting too weak to talk, and his tired body trembled.

In the end of the key rope a big loop had been formed, this after the tent was up, was slipped over a cleat to prevent a possibility of the rope slipping its fastenings and letting the tent down.

Phil had discovered the loop when it finally slipped up so his one hand was pressed against the knot.

Every second the weight on his feet--on his whole body, in fact, was getting heavier.

"If I can hold on a minute longer, I'll make it!" he muttered, his breath coming in short, quick gasps.

What he was seeking to do was to get the rope they had tossed to him, through the big loop. In his effort to do so, the coil slipped from his hands, knocking a canvasman down as it fell, but the lad had held to the other end with a desperate grip.

Now he began working it through the loop inch by inch. It was a slow process, but he was succeeding even better than he had hoped.

Mr. Sparling now saw what Phil's purpose was. About the same time the others down there made the same discovery.

They set up a cheer of approval.

"Wait!" commanded the owner of the show. "The lad isn't out of the woods yet. You men on the net look lively there. If you don't catch him should he fall, you take my word for it, it'll go mighty hard with you."

"We'll catch him."

"You'd better, if you know what's good for you. Goodness, but he's got the strength and the grit! I never saw anything like it in all my circus experience."

They could not help him. There was no way by which any of them could reach Phil, and all they could do was to stand by and do the best they could at breaking his fall should he be forced to let go, as it seemed that he must do soon.

Nearer and nearer crept the line toward the ground, but it was yet far above their heads. It was moving faster, however, as Phil got more weight of rope through the loop, thus requiring less effort on his part to send it along on its journey.

"Side pole! Side pole!" shouted the boy, barely making himself heard above the shouts below.

At first they did not catch the meaning of his words. Mr. Sparling, of course, was the first to do so.

"That's it! Oh, you idiots! You wooden Indians! You thick heads! Get a side pole, don't you understand?" and the owner made a dive at the nearest man to him, whereat the fellow quickly side-stepped and started off on a run for the pole for which Phil had asked. But, even then, some of the hands did not understand what he could want of a side pole.

The instant it was brought Mr. Sparling snatched it from the hands of the tent-man. Raising the pole, assisted by the boss canvasman, he was able to reach the loop. The iron spike in the end of the pole was thrust through the loop, and by exerting considerable pressure they were able to force the loop slowly toward the ground.

"You'll have to hurry! I can't hang on much longer," cried Phil weakly.

"We'll hurry, my lad. It won't be half a minute now," encouraged Mr. Sparling. "Stand by here you blockheads, ready to fall on that rope the minute it gets within reach. Three of you grab hold of the coil end and pay it out gradually. Be careful. Watch your business."

Three men sprang to do his bidding.

"Here comes the loop!"

Ready hands grasped the dangling rope.

The two strands were quickly carried together and the weight of a dozen men thrown on them, instantly relieving the strain on Phil Forrest's body.

Phil had saved the big top, and perhaps a few lives at the same time. Now a sudden dizziness seemed to have overtaken him. Everything appeared to be whirling about him, the big top spinning like a giant top before his eyes.

"Slide down the rope!" commanded Mr. Sparling.

The lad slowly unwound the rope from his arm and feebly motioned to them that they were to walk around the pole with their end so they might hoist the iron ring to the splice of the center pole.

"Never mind anything but yourself!" ordered Mr. Sparling. "We'll attend to this mix-up ourselves."

Very cautiously and deliberately, more from force of habit than otherwise, the lad had let his feet down, and with them was groping for the rope.

"Swing the line between his legs!" roared the owner. "Going to let him stay up there all day?"

"That's what we're trying to do," answered a tentman.

"Yes, I see you trying. That's the trouble with you fellows. You always think you're trying, and if you are, you never accomplish anything. Got, it, Phil?"

"Y--ye--yes."

Twisting his legs about the rope the boy next took a weak grip on it with both hands, then started slowly to descend. This he knew how to do, so the feat was attended with no difficulty other than the strength required, and of which he had none to spare just at the present moment.

"Look out!" he called. He thought he had shouted it in a loud tone. As a matter of fact no sound issued from his lips.

But Mr. Sparling whose eyes had been fixed upon the boy, saw and understood.

"He's falling. Catch him!"

Phil shot downward head first. Yet with the instinct of the showman he curled his head up ever so little as he half consciously felt himself going.

CHAPTER VI
THE SHOWMAN'S REWARD

P hil struck the net with a violent slap that was heard outside the big top, though those without did not understand the meaning of it, nor did they give it heed.

Mr. Sparling was the first to reach him. The lad had landed on his shoulders and then struck flat on his back, the proper way to fall into a net. Perhaps it was instinct that told him what to do.

The lad was unconscious when the showman lifted him tenderly from the net and laid him out on the ground.

"Up with that peak!" commanded Mr. Sparling. "Get some water here, and don't crowd around him! Give the boy air! Tucker, you hike for the surgeon."

A shove started Teddy for the surgeon. In the meantime Mr. Sparling was working over Phil, seeking to bring him back to consciousness, which he finally succeeded in doing before the surgeon arrived.

"Did I fall?" asked Phil, suddenly opening his eyes.

"A high dive," nodded Mr. Sparling.

Phil cast his eyes up to the dome where he saw the canvas drawing taut. He knew that he had succeeded and he smiled contentedly.

By the time the surgeon arrived the boy was on his feet.

"How do you feel?"

"I'm a little sore, Mr. Sparling. But I guess I'll be fit in a few minutes."

"Able to walk over to my tent? If not, I'll have some of the fellows carry you."

"Oh, no; I can walk if I can get my legs started moving. They don't seem to be working the way they should this morning," laughed the lad. "My, that tent weighs something doesn't it?"

"It does," agreed the showman.

Just then the surgeon arrived. After a brief examination he announced that Phil was not injured, unless, perhaps, he might have injured himself internally by subjecting himself to the great strain of holding up the tent.

"I think some breakfast will put me right again," decided the lad.

"Haven't you had your breakfast yet?" demanded Mr. Sparling.

"No; I guess I've been too busy."

"Come with me, then. I haven't had mine either," said the showman.

Linking his arm within that of the Circus Boy, Mr. Sparling walked from the tent, not speaking again until they had reached the manager's private tent. This was a larger and much more commodious affair than it had been last year.

He placed Phil in a folding easy chair, and sat down to his desk where he began writing.

After finishing, Mr. Sparling looked up.

"Phil," he said in a more kindly tone than the lad had ever before heard him use, "I was under a deep obligation to you last season. I'm under a greater one now."

"I wish you wouldn't speak of it, sir. What I have done is purely in the line of duty. It's a fellow's business to be looking out for his employer's interests. That's what I have always tried to do."

"Not only tried, but have," corrected Mr. Sparling. "That's an old-fashioned idea of yours. It's a pity young men don't feel more that way, these days. But that wasn't what I wanted to say. As a little expression of how much I appreciate your interest, as well as the actual money loss you have saved me, I want to make you a little present."

"Oh, no no," protested Phil.

"Here is a check which I have made out for a hundred dollars. That will give you a little start on the season. But it isn't all that I am going to do for you--"

"Please, Mr. Sparling. Believe me I do appreciate your kindness, but I mustn't take the check. I couldn't take the check."

"Why not?"

"Because I haven't earned it."

"Haven't earned it? He hasn't earned it!"

"No, sir."

The showman threw his hands above his head in a hopeless sort of a way.

"I should not feel that I was doing right. I want to be independent, Mr. Sparling. I have plenty of money. I have not spent more than half of what I earned last summer. This season I hope to lay by a whole lot, so that I shall be quite independent."

"And so you shall, so you shall, my boy," Sparling exclaimed, rising and smiting Phil good naturedly with the flat of his hand.

Instead of tearing up the check, however, Mr. Sparling put it in an envelope which he directed and stamped, then thrust in his coat pocket.

"I--I hope you understand--hope you do not feel offended," said Phil hesitatingly. "I should not like to have you misunderstand me."

"Not a bit of it, my lad. I can't say that I have any higher opinion of you because of your decision, but--"

Phil glanced up quickly.

"I already have as high an opinion of you as it is possible for me to have for any human being, and--"

"Thank you. You'll make me have a swelled head if you keep on that way," laughed Phil.

"No danger. You would have had one long ago, if that was your makeup. Have you seen Mrs. Sparling yet?"

"No, and I should like to. May I call on her in your car?"

"Not only may, but she has commissioned me to ask you to. I think we had better be moving over to the cook tent, now, if we wish any breakfast. I expect the hungry roustabouts have about cleaned the place out by this time."

They soon arrived at the cook tent. Here Phil left Mr. Sparling while he passed about among the tables, greeting such of his old acquaintances as he had not yet seen that morning. He was introduced to many of the new ones, all of whom had heard pretty much everything about Phil's past achievements before he reached their tables. The people of a circus are much like a big family, and everyone knows, or thinks he knows, the whole family history of his associates.

Even Phil's plucky work in the big top, less than an hour before, had already traveled to the cook tent, and many curious glances were directed to the slim, modest, boy as he passed among his friends quietly, giving them his greetings.

Teddy, on the other hand, was not saying a word. He was busy eating.

"How's your appetite this morning, Teddy?" questioned Phil, sinking down on the bench beside his companion.

"Pretty fair," answered Teddy in a muffled voice. "I began at the top--"

"Top of what?"

"Top of the bill of fare. I've cleaned up everything halfway down the list, and I'm going through the whole bill, even if I have to get up and shake myself down like the miller does a bag of meal."

"Be careful, old chap. Remember you and I have to begin our real work today. We shall want to be in the best of shape for our ring act. You won't, if you fill up as you are doing now," warned Phil.

"Not going to work today."

"What's that?"

"No flying rings today."

"I don't understand."

"No flying rings, I said. Mr. Sparling isn't going to put on our act today."

"How do you know?" asked Phil in some surprise.

"Heard him say so."

"When?"

"Just now."

"Why, I came in with him myself less than ten minutes ago--"

"I know. He stopped right in front of my table here to speak to the ringmaster. Heard him say you were not to be allowed to go on till tomorrow. We don't have to go in the parade today if we don't want to, either. But you are to ride Emperor in the Grand Entry, and I'm to do my stunt on the educated mule."

"Pshaw, I can work today as well as I ever could," said Phil in a disappointed tone. "And I'm going on, too, unless Mr. Sparling gives me distinct orders to the contrary."

Phil got the orders before he had finished his breakfast.

"Believe me, Phil, I know best," said Mr. Sparling, noting the lad's disappointment. "You have had a pretty severe strain this morning, and to go on now with the excitement of the first day added to that, I fear might be too much for you. It might lay you up for some weeks, and we cannot afford to have that happen, you know. I

need you altogether too much for that."

"Very well, sir; it shall be as you wish. I suppose I may go on in the Grand Entry as usual?"

"Oh, yes, if you wish."

"I do."

"Very well; then I'll let Mr. Kennedy know. You had better lie down and rest while the parade is out."

"Thank you; I hardly think that will be necessary. I feel fit enough for work right now."

"Such is youth and enthusiasm," mused the showman, passing on out of the cook tent, once more to go over his arrangements, for there were many details to be looked after on this the first day of the show's season on the road.

Phil called on Mrs. Sparling after breakfast, receiving from the showman's wife a most hospitable welcome. She asked him all about how he had spent the winter, and seemed particularly interested in Mrs. Cahill, who was now the legal guardian of both the boys. Mrs. Sparling already had a letter in her pocket, with the check for one hundred dollars which the showman had drawn for Phil. It was going to Mrs. Cahill to be deposited to the lad's credit, but he would know nothing of this until the close of the season. After he had gone home he would find himself a hundred dollars richer than he thought.

His call finished, Phil went out and rejoined Teddy. Together they started back toward the dressing tent to set their trunks in order and get out such of their costumes as they would need that afternoon and evening. Then again, the dressing tent was really the most attractive part of the show to all the performers. It was here that they talked of their work and life, occasionally practiced new acts of a minor character, and indulged in pranks like a lot of schoolboys at recess time.

As they were passing down along the outside of the big top, Phil noticed several laborers belonging to the show sitting against the side wall sunning themselves. He observed that one of the men was eyeing Teddy and himself with rather more than ordinary interest.

Phil did not give it a second thought, however, until suddenly Teddy gave his arm a violent pinch.

"What is it?"

"See those fellows sitting there?"

"Yes. What of it?"

"One of them is the fellow who ducked me under the water tank back at Germantown."

"You don't say? Which one?"

"Fellow with the red hair. I heard them call him Larry as I passed, or I might not have noticed him particularly. His hair is redder than Rod Palmer's. I should think it would set him on fire."

"It certainly would seem so."

"Mister Larry has got something coming to him good and proper, and he's going to get it, you take my word for that."

Phil laughed good naturedly.

"Please, now, Teddy, forget it. Don't go and get into any more mix-ups. You'll be sending yourself back home first thing you know. Then it will be a difficult matter to get into any other show if you are sent away from this one in disgrace."

"Don't you worry about me. I'll take care of myself. I always do, don't I?"

"I'm afraid I can't agree to that," laughed Phil. "I should say that quite the contrary is the case."

Teddy fell suddenly silent as they walked on in the bright morning light, drinking in the balmy air in long-drawn breaths. Entering the paddock they turned sharply to the left and pushed their way through the canvas curtains into the dressing tent.

"Hurrah for the Circus Boys," shouted someone. "Hello Samson, are you the strong-armed man that held the tent up by your feet?"

"Strong-footed man, you mean," suggested another. "A strong-armed man uses his arms not his feet."

"Come over here and show yourself," shouted another voice.

Phil walked over and stood smilingly before them. Nothing seemed to disturb his persistent good nature.

"Huh, not so much! I guess they stretched that yarn," grunted a new performer.

"I guess not," interposed Mr. Miaco. "I happened to see that stunt pulled off myself. It was the biggest thing I ever saw a man--let alone a boy--get away with."

Then Mr. Miaco went over the scene with great detail, while Phil stole away to his own corner, where he busied himself bending over his trunk to hide his blushes.

But Teddy felt no such emotion. Almost as soon as he entered the dressing tent he began searching about for something. This he soon found. It was a pail, but he appeared to be in a hurry. Picking up the pail he ran with it to the water barrel, that always stands in the dressing tent, filled the pail and skulked out as if he did not desire to attract attention.

Once outside the dressing tent Teddy ran at full speed across the paddock and out into the big top. A few men were working here putting up apparatus for the performers. They gave no heed to the boy with the pail of water.

Teddy ran his eye along the inside of the tent, nodded and went on to the middle section where he turned, climbing the steps to the upper row.

Arriving there he cautiously peered out over the top of the side wall. What he saw evidently was not to his liking, for once more he picked up the pail of water and ran lightly along the top seat toward the menagerie tent.

All at once he paused, put down his pail and peered out over the side wall again. Nodding with satisfaction he picked up the pail, lifted it to the top of the side wall, once more looked out measuring the distance well, then suddenly turned the pail bottom side up.

In his course through the big top Teddy had gathered up several handfuls of sawdust and dirt which he had stirred well into the water as he ran, making a pasty mess of it.

It was this mixture that he had now poured out over the side wall. Teddy waited only an instant to observe the effect of the deluge that he had turned on. Then he fled down the rattling board seats.

Outside a sudden roar broke the stillness. No sooner had he reached the bottom of the seats than several men raised up the side wall and came tumbling in, yelling like Comanche Indians. Teddy cast one frightened look at them, then ran like all possessed. What he had seen was a red-haired man in the lead, dripping wet with hair and clothes plastered with mud and sawdust. Larry was after the lad in full cry.

CHAPTER VII
TRYING THE CULPRIT

S top him!" howled Larry, as he, followed by half a dozen blue-shirted fellows, bolted into the arena in pursuit of the lad who had emptied the pail of muddy water over him.

Teddy, still clinging to the pail, was sprinting down the concourse as if his very life depended upon it. A canvasman, hearing Larry's call, and suspecting the boy was wanted for something quite serious, rushed out, heading Teddy off. It looked as if the lad were to be captured right here.

But Teddy Tucker was not yet at the end of his resources. He ran straight on as if he had not observed the canvasman. Just as he reached the man, and the latter's hands were stretched out to intercept him, Teddy hurled the pail full in the fellow's face. Then the lad darted to one side and fled toward the paddock.

The canvasman had joined the procession by this time. Into the dressing tent burst the boy, followed by Larry, the others having brought up sharply just before reaching the dressing room, knowing full well that they had no business there and that their presence would be quickly and effectively resented. Larry, consumed with rage, did not stop to think about this, so he dashed on blindly to his fate.

At first the circus performers in the dressing tent could not imagine what was going on. Clotheslines came down, properties were upset and in a moment the tent was in confusion.

"Stop that!" bellowed an irate performer.

Larry gave no heed to the command, and Teddy was in too big a hurry to stop to explain.

Suddenly Phil Forrest, realizing that his little companion was in danger, gave a leap. He landed on Larry's back, pinioning the fellow's arms to his sides.

"You stop that now! You let him alone!" commanded Phil.

Before the canvasman could make an effort to free himself, Mr. Miaco, the head clown, took a hand in the proceedings. Throwing Phil from the tentman, Miaco jerked Larry about, and demanded to know what he meant by intruding on the privacy of the dressing tent in that manner.

"I want that kid," he growled.

"Put him out!" howled a voice.

"What do you want him for?"

"He--he dumped a pail of water over me. I'll get even with him. I'll--"

"How about this, Master Teddy?" questioned Mr. Miaco.

Teddy explained briefly how the fellow Larry and a companion had ducked him under the water tank, and had ruined his clothes, together with causing him to miss his train.

"This demands investigation," decided Mr. Miaco gravely. "Fellows, it is evident that we had better try this man. That is the best way to dispose of his case."

"Yes, yes; try him!" they shouted.

"Whom shall we have for judge?"

"Oscar, the midget!"

The Smallest Man on Earth was quickly boosted to the top of a property box.

"Vot iss?" questioned the midget, his wizened, yellow little face wrinkling into a questioning smile.

"We are going to try this fellow, Larry, and you are to be the judge."

"Yah," agreed Oscar, after which he subsided, listening to the proceedings that followed, with grave, expressionless eyes. It is doubtful if Oscar understood what it was all about, but his gravity and judicial manner sent the whole dressing tent into an uproar of merriment.

After the evidence was all in, the entire company taking part in testifying, amid much merriment--for the performers entered into the spirit of the trial like a lot of schoolboys--Oscar was asked to decide what should be done with the prisoner Larry.

Oscar was at a loss to know how to answer.

"Duck him," suggested one.

This was an inspiration to Oscar. He smiled broadly.

"Yah, dat iss."

"What iss?" demanded the Tallest Man On Earth. "Talk United States."

"Yah," agreed Oscar, smiling seraphically. "Duck um."

"Larry, it is the verdict of this court that you be ducked, as the only fitting punishment for one who has committed the crime of laying hands on a Circus Boy. Are we all agreed on the punishment meted out by the dignified judge?"

"Yes, yes!" they shouted. "The rain barrel for him."

"Men, do your duty!" cried Mr. Miaco.

"I wouldn't do that," interposed Phil. "You haven't any more right to duck him than he had to put Teddy under the water tank. It isn't right."

But they gave no heed to his protests. Willing hands grabbed the red-headed tentman, whose kicks and struggles availed him nothing. Raising him over the barrel of water they soused him in head first, ducking him again and again.

"Take him out. You'll drown him," begged Phil.

Then they hauled Larry out, shaking the water out of him. As soon as his coughing ceased, he threatened dire vengeance against his assailants.

Four performers then carried their victim to the opening of the dressing tent and threw him out bodily.

Instantly Larry's companions saw him fall at their feet, and heard his angry explanation of the indignities that had been heaped upon him. There was a lively scrambling over the ground, and the next instant a volley of stones was hurled into the dressing tent.

Phil was just coming out on his way to the main entrance as the row began. A stone just grazed his cheek. Without giving the least heed to the assailants, he turned to cross the paddock in order to slip out under the tent and go on about his business. Most lads would have run under the circumstances. Not so Phil. His were steady nerves.

"There he is! Grab him!" shouted Larry, catching sight of Phil and charging that Phil had been one of those who had helped duck him.

Such was not the case, however, for instead of having taken part in the ducking, Phil Forrest had tried to prevent it.

Larry and another man were running toward him. The lad halted, turned and faced them.

"What do you want of me?" he demanded.

"I'll show you what I want of you. You started this row."

"I did nothing of the sort, sir. You go on about your business and I shall do the same, whether you do or not."

Phil raised the canvas and stepped out. But no sooner had he gotten out into the lot than the two men burst through the flapping side wall.

The boy saw them coming and knew that he was face to face with trouble.

He adopted a ruse, knowing full well that he could not hope to cope with the brawny canvasmen single handed and alone. Starting off on a run, Phil was followed instantly, as he felt sure he would be, but managing to keep just ahead of the men and no more.

"I've got you!"

The voice was almost at his ear.

Phil halted with unexpected suddenness and dropped on all fours.

The canvasman was too close to check his own speed. He fell over Phil, landing on his head and shoulders in the dirt.

The lad was up like a flash. Larry was close upon him now, and with a snarl of rage launched a blow full at Phil Forrest's face. But he had not reckoned on the lad's agility, nor did he know that Phil was a trained athlete. Therefore, Larry's surprise was great when his fist beat the empty air.

Thrown off his balance, Larry measured his length on the ground.

"I advise you to let me alone," warned Phil coolly, as the tentman was scrambling to his feet. Already Larry's companion had gotten up and was gazing at Phil in a half dazed sort of way.

"Get hold of him, Bad Eye! What are you standing there like a dummy for? He'll run in a minute."

Phil's better judgment told him to do that very thing, but he could not bring himself to run from danger. Much as he disliked a row, he was too plucky and courageous to run from danger.

Bad Eye was rushing at him, his eyes blazing with anger.

Phil side-stepped easily, avoiding his antagonist without the least difficulty. But now he had to reckon with Larry, who, by this time, had gotten to his feet.

It was two to one.

"Stand back unless you want to get hurt!" cried Phil, with a warning glint in his eyes.

Larry, by way of answer, struck viciously at him. Phil, with a glance about him, saw that he could not expect help, for there was no one in sight, the performers being engaged at that moment in driving off the angry laborers, which they were succeeding in doing with no great effort on their part.

The lad cleverly dodged the blow. But instead of backing away as the canvasman's fist barely grazed his cheek, Phil, with a short arm jolt, caught his adversary on the point of his chin. Larry instantly lost all desire for fight. He sat down on the hard ground with a bump.

Now Bad Eye rushed in. Again Phil sidestepped, and, thrusting a foot between the fellow's legs, tripped him neatly.

Half a dozen men came running from the paddock. They were the fellows whom the performers had put to rout. At that moment the bugle blew for all hands to prepare for the parade.

"I guess I have done about enough for one day," decided Phil. "And for a sick man it wasn't a half bad job."

With an amused glance at his fallen adversaries Phil ran to the big top, less than a rod away, and, lifting the sidewall, slipped under and disappeared within.

CHAPTER VIII
PHIL MAKES A NEW FRIEND

Tweetle! Tweetle!"

Two rippling blasts from the ringmaster's whistle notified the show people that the performance was on. In moved the procession for the Grand Entry, as the silken curtains separating the paddock from the big top slowly fell apart.

Phil, from his lofty perch on the head of old Emperor, peering through the opening of the bonnet in which he was concealed, could not repress an exclamation of admiration. It was a splendid spectacle--taken from a story of ancient Rome--that was sweeping majestically about the arena to the music of an inspiring tune into which the big circus band had suddenly launched.

Gayly-caparisoned, nervous horses pranced and reared; huge wagons, gorgeous under their coat of paint and gold, glistened in the afternoon sunlight that fell softly through the canvas top and gave the peculiar rattling sound so familiar to the lover of the circus as they moved majestically into the arena; elephants trumpeted shrilly and the animals back in the menagerie tent sent up a deafening roar of protest. After months of quiet in their winter quarters, this unusual noise and excitement threw the wild beasts into a tempest of anger. Pacing their cages with upraised heads, they hurled their loud-voiced protests into the air until the more timid of the spectators trembled in their seats.

It was an inspiring moment for the circus people, as well as for the spectators.

"Tweetle! Tweetle!" sang the ringmaster's whistle after the spectacle had wound its way once around the concourse.

At this the procession wheeled, its head cutting between the two rings, slowly and majestically reaching for the paddock and dressing tent, where the performers would hurry into their costumes for their various acts to follow.

This left only the elephants in the ring. The huge beasts now began their evolutions, ponderous but graceful, eliciting great applause, as did their trainer, Mr. Kennedy. Then came the round-off of the act. This, it will be remembered, was of Phil Forrest's own invention, the act in which Phil, secreted in the elephant's bonnet, burst out at the close of the act, and, by the aid of wires running over a pulley above him, was able to descend gracefully to the sawdust arena.

He was just a little nervous in this, the first performance of the season, but, steadying his nerves, he went through the act without a hitch and amid thunders of applause. As in the previous season's act, old Emperor carried the lad from the ring, holding Phil out in front of him firmly clasped in his trunk. No similar act ever had been seen in a circus until Phil and Emperor worked it out for themselves. It had become one of the features of the show last year, and it bade fair to be equally popular that season. Phil had added to it somewhat, which gave the act much more finish than before.

"Very good, young man," approved Mr. Sparling, as the elephant bore the lad out. Mr. Sparling was watching the show with keen eyes in order to decide what necessary changes were to be made. "Coming back to watch the performance?"

"Oh, yes. I wouldn't miss that for anything."

As soon as the lad had thrown off his costume and gotten back into his clothes, he hurried into the big top, where he found Teddy, who did not go on in his bucking mule act until later.

"How's the show, Teddy?" greeted Phil.

"Great. Greatest thing I ever saw. Did you see the fellows jump over the herd of elephants and horses?"

"No. Who were they?"

"Oh, most all of the crowd, I guess. I'm going to do that."

"You, Teddy? Why, you couldn't jump over half a dozen elephants and turn a somersault. You would break your neck the first thing."

"Mr. Miaco says I could. Says I'm just the build for that sort of thing," protested the lad.

"Well, then, get him to teach you. Of course we can't know how to do too many things in this business. We have learned that it pays to know how to do almost everything. Have you made friends with the mule since you got back?"

"Yes. He spooned over me and made believe he loved me like a brother."

Teddy paused reflectively.

"Then what?"

"Well, then he tried to kick the daylight out of me."

"I thought so," laughed Phil. "I'm glad I chose an elephant for my friend, instead of an educated mule. When are you going to begin on the springboard--begin practicing, I mean?"

"Mr. Miaco says he'll teach me as soon as we get settled--"

"Settled? I never heard of a show getting settled--that is, not until the season is ended and it is once more in winter quarters. I suppose by 'settled' he means when everything gets to moving smoothly."

"I guess so," nodded Teddy. "What are you going to do?"

"The regular acts that I did last year."

"No; I mean what are you going to learn new?"

"Oh! Well, there are two things I'm crazy to be able to do."

"What are they?"

"One is to be a fine trapeze performer," announced Phil thoughtfully.

"And the other?"

"To ride bareback."

"Want to be the whole thing, don't you?" jeered Teddy.

"No; not quite. But I should like to be able to do those two things, and to do them well. There is nothing that catches the audiences as do the trapezists and the bareback riders. And it fascinates me as well."

"Here, too," agreed Teddy.

"But there is one thing I want to talk with you about--to read you a lecture."

"You needn't."

"I shouldn't be surprised if there was some sort of an inquiry about the row in the dressing tent. You know Mr. Sparling won't stand for anything of that sort."

"He doesn't know about it," interposed Teddy.

"But we do. Therefore, we are just as much to blame as if he did know. And I am not so sure that he doesn't. You can't fool Mr. Sparling. You ought to know that by this time. There isn't a thing goes on in this show that he doesn't find out about, sooner or later, and he is going to find out about this."

"I didn't do anything. You did, when you had a scrap with those two fellows out on the lot."

"You forget that you started the row by emptying a pail of water on Larry's head. Don't you call that starting doing anything? I do."

Phil had to laugh at the comical expression on his companion's face.

"Well, maybe."

"And we haven't heard the last of those fellows yet. They're mad all through. I am sorry I had to hit them. But they would have used me badly had I not done something to protect myself. I should tell the whole matter to Mr. Sparling, were it not that I would get others into trouble. That I wouldn't do."

"I should think not."

"By the way, Teddy, there come the bareback riders. Don't you follow after their act?"

"My! That's so. I had forgotten all about that. Thought I was watching the show just like the rest of the folks."

"Better hustle, or you won't get into your makeup in time to go on. There'll be a row for certain if you are late."

But Teddy already had started on a run for the dressing tent, bowling over a clown at the entrance to the paddock and bringing down the wrath of that individual as he hustled for the dressing tent and began feverishly getting into his ring clothes. These consisted of a loose fitting pair of trousers, a slouch hat and a coat much the worse for wear. A "Rube" act, it was called in show parlance, and it was that in very truth, more because of Teddy's drollery than for the makeup that he wore.

Phil quickly forgot all about the lecture he had been reading to his companion as the bareback riders came trotting in. His eyes were fixed on a petite, smiling figure who tripped up to the curbing, where she turned toward the audience, and, kicking one foot out behind her, bowed and threw a kiss to the spectators.

Phil had walked over and sat down by the center pole right near the sawdust ring, so that he might get a better view of the riding.

The young woman who so attracted his attention was known on the show bills as "Little Miss Dimples, the Queen of the Sawdust Arena." Phil, as he gazed at her graceful little figure, agreed that the show bills did not exaggerate her charms at all.

Little Dimples, using the ringmaster's hand as a step, vaulted lightly to the back of the great gray ring horse, where she sat as the animal began a slow walk about the ring.

Phil wondered how she could stay on, for she appeared to be sitting right on the animal's sloping hip.

The band struck up a lively tune, the gray horse began a slow, methodical gallop. The first rise of the horse bounded Little Dimples to her knees, and the next to her feet.

With a merry little "yip! yip!" she began executing a fairy-like dance, keeping time with her whip, which she held grasped in both hands.

"Beautiful!" cried Phil, bringing his hands together sharply. In fact, he had never seen such artistic riding. The girl seemed to be treading on air, so lightly did her feet touch the rosined back of the ring horse.

Little Dimples heard and understood. She flashed a brilliant smile at Phil and tossed her whip as a salute. Phil had never met her, but they both belonged to the same great family, and that was sufficient.

His face broke out into a pleased smile at her recognition and the lad touched his hat lightly, settling back against the center pole to watch Dimples' riding, which had only just begun. It made him laugh outright to see her big picture hat bobbing up and down with the motion of the horse.

"Works just like an elephant's ear when the flies are thick," was the lad's somewhat inelegant comparison.

But now Dimples removed the hat, sending it spinning to the ringmaster, who, in turn, tossed it to an attendant. The real work of the act was about to start. Phil never having seen the young woman ride, did not know what her particular specialty was. Just now he was keenly observing, that he might learn her methods.

Dimples' next act was to jump through a series of paper hoops. This finished, she leaped to the ring, and, taking a running start, vaulted to the back of her horse.

"Bravo!" cried Phil, which brought another brilliant smile from the rider. She knew that it was not herself, but her work, that had brought this expression of approval from the Circus Boy, whom she already knew of by hearing some of the other performers tell of his achievements since he joined the circus less than a year ago.

"The ring is rough. I should have thought they would have leveled it down better," Phil grumbled, noting the uneven surface of the sawdust circle with critical eyes. "I'll bet Mr. Sparling hasn't seen that, or he would have raised a row. But still Dimples seems very sure on her feet. I wonder if she does any brilliant stunts?"

As if in answer to the lad's question, the "tweetle" of the ringmaster's whistle brought everything to a standstill under the big top. Even the band suddenly ceased playing. Then Phil knew that something worthwhile was coming.

"Ladies and gentlemen!" announced the ringmaster, holding up his right hand to attract the eyes of the spectators to him, "Little Miss Dimples, The Queen of the Sawdust Arena, will now perform her thrilling, death-defying, unexcelled, unequaled feat of turning a somersault on the back of a running horse. I might add in this connection that Little Miss Dimples is the only woman who ever succeeded in going through this feat without finishing up by breaking her neck. The band will cease playing while this perilous performance is on, as the least distraction on the part of the rider might result fatally for her. Ladies and gentlemen, I introduce to you Little Miss Dimples," concluded the ringmaster, with a comprehensive wave of the hand toward the young woman and her gray ring horse.

Dimples dropped to the ring, swept a courtesy to the audience, then leaped to the animal's back with a sharp little "yip! yip!"

During the first round of the ring she removed the bridle, tossing it mischievously in Phil's direction. He caught it deftly, placing it on the ground beside him, then edged a little closer to the ring that he might the better observe her work.

The ring horse started off at a lively gallop, the rider allowing her elbows to rise and fall with the motion of the horse, in order that she might the more thoroughly become a part of the animal itself--that the motion of each should be the same.

Suddenly Dimples sprang nimbly to her feet, tossing her riding whip to the waiting hands of the ringmaster.

Phil half scrambled to his feet as he saw her poise for a backward somersault. He had noted another thing, too. She was going to throw herself, it seemed, just as the horse was on the roughest part of the ring. He wondered if she could make it. To him it was a risky thing to try, but she no doubt knew better than he what she was about.

The ringmaster held up his hand as a signal to the audience that the daring act was about to take place.

Phil crept a little nearer.

All at once the girl gracefully threw herself into the air. He judged she had cleared the back of the animal by at least three feet, a high jump to make straight up with unbent knees.

But just as she was leaving the back of the horse, the animal suddenly stumbled, thus turning her halfway around, and for the instant taking her mind from her work. Dimples already had begun to turn backward, but he noted that all at once she stopped turning.

Phil knew what that meant. As show people term it, she had "frozen" in the air. She was falling, head first, right toward the wooden ring curbing.

"Turn! Turn!" cried Phil sharply.

The girl was powerless to do so, while the ringmaster, being on the opposite side of the ring, could be of no assistance to her.

"Turn!" shouted Phil, more loudly this time, giving a mighty spring in the direction of the falling woman.

CHAPTER IX
THE MULE DISTINGUISHES HIMSELF

The audience had half risen, believing that the girl would surely be killed. It did seem that it would be a miracle if she escaped without serious injury. But the Circus Boy, his every faculty centered on the task before him, proposed to save her if he could.

He sprang up on the ring curbing, stretching both hands above his head as far as he could reach, bracing himself with legs wide apart to meet the shock.

It is not an easy task to attempt to catch a person, especially if that person be falling toward you head first. But Phil Forrest calculated in a flash how he would do it. That is, he would unless he missed.

It all happened in much less time than it takes to tell it, of course, and a moment afterwards one could not have told how it had occurred.

The Circus Boy threw both hands under Dimples' outstretched arms with the intention of jerking her down to her feet, then springing from the curbing with her before both should topple over.

His plan worked well up to the point of catching her. But instantly upon doing so he realized that she was moving with such speed as to make it impossible for him to retain his balance.

Dimples was hurled into his arms with great force, bowling Phil over like a ninepin. Yet, in falling, he did not lose his presence of mind. He hoped fervently that he might be fortunate enough not to strike on a stake, of which there were many on that side of the ring.

"Save yourself!" gasped the girl.

Instead, Phil held her up above him at arm's length. When he struck it was full on his back, the back of his head coming in contact with the hard ground with such

force as to stun him almost to the point of unconsciousness. As he struck he gave Dimples a little throw so that she cleared his body, landing on the ground beyond him.

The girl stretched forth her hands and did a handspring, once more thorough master of herself, landing gracefully on her feet. But Phil had undoubtedly saved her life, as she well knew.

Without giving the slightest heed to the audience, which was howling its delight, Dimples ran to the fallen lad, leaning over him anxiously.

"Are you hurt?" she begged, placing a hand on his head.

"I--I guess not," answered Phil, pulling himself together a little. "I'll get up or they'll think something is the matter with me."

"Let me help you."

"No, thank you," he replied, brushing aside the hand she had extended to him. But his back hurt him so severely that he could only with difficulty stand upright.

Phil smiled and straightened, despite the pain.

At that Dimples grasped him by the hand, leading him to the concourse facing the reserved seats, where she made a low bow to the audience; then, throwing both arms about Phil, she gave him a hearty kiss.

Thunders of applause greeted this, the audience getting to its feet in its excitement. Had it been possible, both the boy and Miss Dimples would have been borne in triumph from the ring.

"Come back and sit down while I finish my act," she whispered.

"You're not going to try that again, are you?" questioned Phil.

"Of course I am. You'll see what a hit it will make."

"I saw that you came near making a hit a few moments ago," answered the lad.

"There, there; don't be sarcastic," she chided, giving him a playful tap. "If you feel strong enough, please help me up."

Phil did so smilingly; then he retired to his place by the center pole, against which he braced his aching back.

"Turn after you have gotten over the rough spot," he cautioned her.

Dimples nodded her understanding.

This time Phil held his breath as he saw her crouching ever so little for her spring.

Dimples uttered another shrill "yip!" and threw herself into the air again.

He saw, with keen satisfaction, that this time she was not going to miss. Dimples turned in the air with wonderful grace, alighting far back on the broad hips of the gray horse with bird-like lightness.

Phil doffed his hat, and, getting to his feet, limped away, with the audience roaring out its applause. They had forgotten all about the boy who but a few moments before had saved Little Dimples' life, and he was fully as well satisfied that it should be so.

Just as he was passing the bandstand the educated mule, with Teddy Tucker on its back, bolted through the curtains like a projectile. The mule nearly ran over Phil, then brought up suddenly to launch both heels at him. But the Circus Boy had seen this same mule in action before, and this time Phil had discreetly ducked under the bandstand.

Then the mule was off.

"Hi-yi-yi-yip-yi!" howled Teddy, as the outfit bolted into the arena. The old hands with the show discreetly darted for cover when they saw Teddy and his mule coming. Like Phil Forrest, they had had experience with this same wild outfit before. There was no knowing what the bucking mule might not do, while there was a reasonable certainty in their minds as to what he would do if given half a chance.

"Hi! Hi! Look out!" howled Teddy as they neared the entrance to the menagerie tent, where a number of people were standing. The boy saw that the mule had taken it into his stubborn head to enter the menagerie tent, there to give an exhibition of his contrariness.

In they swept like a miniature whirlwind, the mule twisting this way and that, stopping suddenly now and then and bracing its feet in desperate efforts to unseat its rider.

But Teddy held on grimly. This rough riding was the delight of his heart, and the lad really was a splendid horseman, though it is doubtful if he realized this fact himself.

A man was crossing the menagerie tent with a pail of water in each hand. The mule saw him. Here was an opportunity not to be lost.

Teddy's mount swept past the fellow. Then both the beast's heels shot out, catching both the pails at the same time. The two pails took the air in a beautiful curve, like a pair of rockets, distributing water all the way across the tent, a liberal portion of which was spilled over the water carrier as the pails left his hands.

The man chanced to be Larry, Teddy's enemy. Teddy was traveling at such a rapid rate that he did not recognize the fellow, but Larry recognized him, and thereby another account was charged up against the Circus Boy.

But the mule, though the time limit for his act had expired, had not quite satisfied his longing for excitement. Whirling about, he plunged toward the big top again.

"Whoa! Whoa!" howled Teddy, tugging at the reins. But he might as well have tried to check the wind. Nothing short of a stone wall could stop the educated mule until he was ready to stop. The ringmaster had blown his whistle for the next act and the performers were running to their stations when Teddy and his mount suddenly made their appearance again.

"Get out of here!" yelled the ringmaster.

"I am trying to do so," howled Teddy in a jeering voice. "Can't go any faster than I am."

"Stop him! You'll run somebody down!" shouted Mr. Sparling, dodging out of the way as the mule, with ears laid back on his head, dashed straight at the showman.

"Can't stop. In a hurry," answered Teddy.

On they plunged past the bandstand again, the mule pausing at the paddock entrance long enough to kick the silk curtains into ribbons. Next he made a dive for the dressing tent.

In less time than it takes to tell it, the dressing tent looked as if it had been struck by a cyclone.

Clubs and side poles were brought down on the rump of the wild mule, most of which were promptly kicked through the side of the tent. Teddy, in the meantime, had landed in a performer's trunk, smashing through the tray, being wedged in so tightly that he could not extricate himself. Added to the din was Teddy's voice howling for help.

The performers, in all stages of dress and undress, had fled to the outside.

Then, the mule becoming suddenly meek, pricked forward his ears, ambled out into the paddock and began contentedly nibbling at the fresh grass about the edges of the enclosure.

About this time Mr. Sparling came running in. His face was red and the perspiration was rolling down it.

"Where's that fool boy?" he bellowed. "Where is he, I say?"

"Here he is," answered the plaintive voice of Teddy Tucker.

"Come out of that!"

"I can't. I'm stuck fast."

The showman jerked him out with scant ceremony, while Teddy began pulling pieces of the trunk tray out of his clothes.

"Do you want to put my show out of business? What do you think this is--a cowboy picnic? I'll fire you. I'll--"

"Better fire the mule. I couldn't stop him," answered the boy.

By this time the performers, after making sure that the mule had gone, were creeping back.

"I'll cut that act out. I'll have the mule shot. I'll-- Get out of here, before I take you over my knee and give you what you deserve."

"I'm off," grinned Teddy, ducking under the canvas.

He was seen no more about the dressing tent until just before it was time to go on for the evening performance.

CHAPTER X
HIS FIRST BAREBACK LESSON

Where's that boy?"

"He'll catch it if he ever dares show his face in this dressing tent again."

This and other expressions marked the disapproval of the performers of the manner in which their enclosure had been entered and disrupted.

"Don't blame him; blame the mule," advised Mr. Miaco, the head clown.

"Yes; Teddy wasn't to blame," declared Phil, who had entered at that moment. "Did he do all this?" he asked, looking about at the scene of disorder.

"He did. Lucky some of us weren't killed," declared one. "If that mule isn't cut out of the programme I'll quit this outfit. Never safe a minute while he and the kid are around. First, the kid gets us into a scrimmage with the roustabouts, then he slam bangs into the dressing tent with a fool mule and puts the whole business out of the running."

"Was Mr. Sparling--was he mad?" asked Phil, laughing until the tears started.

"Mad? He was red headed," replied Miaco.

"Where's Teddy?"

"He got stuck in the strong man's trunk there. The boss had to pull him out, for he was wedged fast. Then the young man prudently made his escape. If the boss hadn't skinned him we would have done so. He got out just in time."

"Are you Phil Forrest?" asked a uniformed attendant entering the dressing tent.

"Yes; what is it?"

"Lady wants to see you out in the paddock."

"Who is it?"

"Mrs. Robinson."

"I don't know any Mrs. Robinson."

"He means Little Dimples," Mr. Miaco informed him.

"Oh."

Phil hurried from the tent. Dimples was sitting on a property box, industriously engaged on a piece of embroidery work. She made a pretty picture perched up on the box engaged in her peaceful occupation with the needle, and the lad stopped to gaze at her admiringly.

Dimples glanced down with a smile.

"Does it surprise you to see me at my fancy work? That's what I love. Why, last season, I embroidered a new shirt waist every week during the show season. I don't know what I'll do with them all. But come over here and sit down by me. I ought to thank you for saving my life this afternoon, but I know you would rather I did not."

Phil nodded.

"I don't like to be thanked. It makes me feel--well, awkward, I guess. You froze, didn't you?"

"I did," and Dimples laughed merrily.

"What made you do so--the horse?"

"Yes. I thought he was going to fall all the way down, then by the time I remembered where I was I couldn't turn to save my life. I heard you call to me to do so, but I couldn't. But let's talk about you. You hurt your back, didn't you?"

"Nothing to speak of. It will be all right by morning. I'm just a little lame now. Where were you--what show were you with last year?"

"The Ringlings."

"The Ringlings?" marveled Phil. "Why, I shouldn't think you would want to leave a big show like that for a little one such as this?"

"It's the price, my dear boy. I get more money here, and I'm a star here. In the big shows one is just a little part of a big organization. There's nothing like the small shows for comfort and good fellowship. Don't you think so?"

"I don't know," admitted Phil. "This is the only show I have ever been with. I 'joined out' last season--"

"Only last season? Well, well! I must say you have made pretty rapid progress for one who has been out less than a year."

"I have made a lot of blunders," laughed Phil. "But I'm learning. I wish, though, that I could do a bareback act one quarter as well as you do. I should be very proud if I could."

"Have you ever tried it?"

"No."

"Why don't you learn, then? You'd pick it up quickly."

"For the reason that I have never had an opportunity--I've had no one to teach me."

"Then you shall do so now. Your teacher is before you."

"You--you mean that you will teach me?"

"Of course. What did you think I meant?"

"I--I wasn't sure. That will be splendid."

"I saw your elephant act. You are a very finished performer-- a natural born showman. If you stay in the business long enough you will make a great reputation for yourself."

"I don't want to be a performer all my life. I am going to own a show some of these days," announced the boy confidently.

"Oh, you are, are you?" laughed Dimples. "Well, if you say so, I most surely believe you. You have the right sort of pluck to get anything you set your heart on. Now if my boy only--"

"Your boy?"

"Yes. Didn't you know that I am a married woman?"

"Oh my, I thought you were a young girl," exclaimed Phil.

"Thank you; that was a very pretty compliment. But, alas, I am no longer young. I have a son almost as old as you are. He is with his father, performing at the Crystal Palace in London. I expect to join them over there after my season closes here."

"Is it possible?"

"Yes, and as my own boy is so far away I shall have to be a sort of mother to you this season. You have no mother, have you?"

"No. My mother is dead," answered the lad in a low voice, lowering his eyes.

"I thought as much. Mothers don't like to have their boys join a circus; but, if they knew what a strict, wholesome life a circus performer has to lead, they would not be so set against the circus. Don't you think, taking it all in all, that we are a pretty good sort?" smiled Dimples.

"I wish everyone were as good as circus folks," the boy made answer so earnestly as to bring a pleased smile to the face of his companion.

"You shall have a lesson today for that, if you wish."

"Do I?"

"Then run along and get on your togs. As soon as the performance is over we will get out my ring horse and put in an hour's work."

"Thank you, thank you!" glowed Phil as Mrs. Robinson rolled up her work. "I'll be out in a few moments."

Full of pleasurable anticipation, Phil ran to the dressing tent and began rummaging in his trunk for his working tights. These he quickly donned and hurried back to the paddock. There he found Dimples with her ring horse, petting the broad-backed beast while he nibbled at the grass.

"Waiting, you see?" she smiled up at Forrest.

"Yes. But the performance isn't finished yet, is it?"

"No. The hippodrome races are just going on. Come over to this side of the paddock, where we shall be out of the way, and I'll teach you a few first principles."

"What do you want me to do first?"

"Put your foot in my hand and I will give you a lift."

The lad did as directed and sprang lightly to the back of the gray.

"Move over on the horse's hip. There. Sit over just as far as you can without slipping off. You saw how I did it this afternoon?"

"Yes--oh, here I go!"

Phil slid from the sloping side of the ring horse, landing in a heap, to the accompaniment of a rippling laugh from Dimples.

"I guess I'm not much of a bareback rider," grinned the lad, picking himself up. "How do you manage to stay on it in that position?"

"I don't know. It is just practice. You will catch the trick of it very soon."

"I'm not so sure of that."

"There! Now, take hold of the rein and stand up. Don't be afraid--"

"I'm not. Don't worry about my being afraid."

"I didn't mean it that way. Move back further. It is not good to stand in the middle of your horse's back all the time. Besides throwing too much weight on the back, you are liable to tickle the animal there and make him nervous. The best work is done by standing over the horse's hip. That's it. Tread on the balls of your feet."

But Phil suddenly went sprawling, landing on the ground again, at which both laughed merrily.

Very shortly after that the show in the big top came to a close. The concert was now going on, at the end nearest the menagerie tent, so Phil and Dimples took the ring at the other end of the tent, where they resumed their practice.

After a short time Phil found himself able to stand erect with more confidence. Now, his instructor, with a snap of her little whip, started the gray to walking slowly about the ring, Phil holding tightly to the bridle rein to steady himself.

"Begin moving about now. Tread softly and lightly. That's it. You've caught it already."

"Why not put a pad on the horse's back, as I've seen some performers do?" he questioned.

"No. I don't want you to begin that way. Start without a pad, and you never will have to unlearn what you get. That's my advice. I'm going to set him at a gallop now. Stand straight and lean back a little."

The ring horse moved off at a slow, methodical gallop.

Phil promptly fell off, landing outside the ring, from where he picked himself up rather crestfallen.

"Never mind. You'll learn. You are doing splendidly," encouraged Dimples, assisting him to mount again. "There's the press agent, Mr. Dexter, watching you. Now do your prettiest. Do you know him?"

"No; I have not met him. He's the fellow that Teddy says blows up his words with a bicycle pump."

"That's fine. I shall have to tell him that. Remember, you always want to keep good friends with the press agent. He's the man who makes or unmakes you after you have passed the eagle eyes of the proprietor," Dimples laughed. "From what I hear I guess you stand pretty high with Mr. Sparling."

"I try to do what is right--do the best I know how."

She nodded, clucking to the gray and Phil stopped talking at once, for he was fully occupied in sticking to the horse, over whose back he sprawled every now and then in the most ridiculous of positions. But, before the afternoon's practice had ended, the lad had made distinct progress. He found himself able to stand erect, by the aid of the bridle rein, and to keep his position fairly well while the animal took a slow gallop. He had not yet quite gotten over the dizziness caused by the constant traveling about in a circle in the narrow ring, but Dimples assured him that, after a few more turns, this would wear off entirely.

After finishing the practice, Dimples led her horse back to the horse tent, promising Phil that they should meet the next afternoon.

Phil had no more than changed to his street clothes before he received a summons to go to Mr. Sparling in his private tent.

"I wonder what's wrong now?" muttered the lad. "But, I think I know. It's about that row we had this morning out on the lot. I shouldn't be surprised if I got fined for that."

With a certain nervousness, Phil hurried out around the dressing tent, and skirting the two big tents, sought out Mr. Sparling in his office.

CHAPTER XI
SUMMONED BEFORE THE MANAGER

The lad was not far wrong in his surmise. That Mr. Sparling was angry was apparent at the first glance.

He eyed Phil from head to foot, a fierce scowl wrinkling his face and forehead.

"Well, sir, what have you been up to this afternoon?"

"Practicing in the ring since the afternoon performance closed."

"H-m-m-m! And this forenoon?"

"Not much of anything in the way of work."

"Have any trouble with any of the men?"

"Yes, sir."

"Who?"

"A man by the name of Larry, and another whom they call Bad Eye."

"Humph! I suppose you know it's a bad breach of discipline in a show to have any mixups, don't you?"

"I do. I make no apologies, except that I was acting wholly in self defense. All the same, I do not expect any favoritism. I am willing to take my punishment, whatever it may be," replied the lad steadily.

There was the merest suspicion of a twinkle in the eyes of the showman.

"Tell me what you did."

"I punched Larry, tripped his friend, and--well, I don't exactly know all that did happen," answered Phil without a change of expression.

"Knock them down?"

"I--I guess so."

"H-m-m. I suppose you know both those fellows are pretty bad medicine, don't you?"

"I may have heard something of the sort."

"Larry has quite a reputation as a fighter."

"Yes, sir."

"And you knocked him out?"

"Something like that," answered Phil meekly.

"Show me how you did it?" demanded Mr. Sparling, rising and standing before the culprit.

"It was like this, you see," began Phil, exhibiting a sudden interest in the inquiry. "I was chased by the two men. Suddenly I stopped and let the fellow, Larry, fall over me. During the scrimmage I tripped Bad Eye. I didn't hit anyone until Larry crowded me so I had to do so in order to save myself, or else run away."

"Why didn't you run, young man?"

"I--I didn't like to do that, you know."

Mr. Sparling nodded his head.

"How did you hit him?"

"He made a pass at me like this," and the lad lifted Mr. Sparling's hand over his shoulder. "I came up under his guard with a short arm jolt like this."

"Well, what next?"

"That was about all there was to it. The others came out, about that time, and I ducked in under the big top."

To Phil's surprise Mr. Sparling broke out into a roar of laughter. In a moment he grew sober and stern again.

"Be good enough to tell me what led up to this assault. What happened before that brought on the row? I can depend upon you to give me the facts. I can't say as much for all the others."

Phil did as the showman requested, beginning with the ducking of Teddy by the men when the show was leaving Germantown, and ending with Teddy's having emptied a pail of muddy water over Larry's red head that morning.

He had only just finished his narration of the difficulty, when who should appear at the entrance to the office tent but Larry himself. He was followed, a few paces behind, by Bad Eye.

Mr. Sparling's stern, judicial eyes were fixed upon them. He demanded to hear from them their version of the affair, which Larry related, leaving out all mention of his having ducked Teddy. His story agreed in the main details with what Phil already had said, excepting that Larry's recital threw the blame on Teddy and Phil.

Mr. Sparling took a book from his desk, making a memorandum therein.

"Is that all, sir?" questioned Larry.

"Not quite. If I hear of any further infraction of the rules of this show on the part of either of you two, you close right then. Understand?"

"Yes."

"That's not all; I'll have you both jailed for assault. As it is, I'll fine you both a week's pay. Now get out of here!"

Larry hesitated, flashed a malignant glance at Phil Forrest; then, turning on his heel, he left the tent.

"Don't you think you had better fine me, too, sir?" asked Phil.

"What for?"

"Because I shall have to do it again some of these days."

"What do you mean?"

"That fellow is going to be even with me at the very first opportunity."

Mr. Sparling eyed the lad for a moment.

"I guess you will be able to give a good account of yourself if he tries to do anything of the sort. Let me say right here, though you need not tell your friend so that I think Teddy did just right, and I am glad you gave Larry a good drubbing. But, of course, we can't encourage this sort of thing with the show. It has to be put down with an iron hand."

"I understand, sir."

"Mind, I don't expect you to be a coward."

"I hope not. My father used to teach me not to be. He frequently said, 'Phil, keep out of trouble, but if you get into it, don't sneak out.' "

"That's the talk," roared Mr. Sparling, smiting his desk with a mighty fist. "You run along, now, and give your young friend some advice about what he may expect if he gets into any more difficulty."

"I have done that already."

"Good! Tell it to him again as coming from me. He's going to make a good showman, though he came near putting this outfit out of business with the fool mule this afternoon. I would cut the act out, but for the fact that it is a scream from start to finish. Feeling all right?"

"Yes, thank you. I am perfectly able to go on in the ring act tonight, if you think best."

"Wait until tomorrow; wait until tomorrow. You'll be all the better for it."

The cook tent was open, as Phil observed. The red flag was flying from the center pole of the tent, indicating that supper was being served. In a short time the tent would come down and be on its way in the flying squadron to the next stand.

The show was now less than a day out, but many things had happened. Not a moment had been without its interest or excitement, and Phil realized that as he walked toward the cook tent. He found Teddy there, satisfying his appetite, or rather exerting himself in that direction, for Teddy's appetite was a thing never wholly satisfied.

After supper Phil took the boy aside and delivered Mr. Sparling's message. Teddy looked properly serious, but it is doubtful if the warning sank very deep into his mind, for the next minute he was turning handsprings on the lot.

"Know what I'm going to do, Phil?" he glowed.

"There's no telling what you will do, from one minute to the next, Teddy," replied Phil.

"Going to practice up and see if I can't get in the leaping act."

"That's a good idea. When do you begin taking lessons?"

"Taking 'em now."

"From Mr. Miaco?"

"Yes. I did a turn off the springboard this afternoon with the 'mechanic on,' " meaning the harness used to instruct beginners in the art of tumbling.

"How did you make out?"

"Fine! I'd have broken my neck if it hadn't been for the harness."

Phil laughed heartily.

"I should say you did do finely. But you don't expect to be able to jump over ten elephants and horses the way the others do?"

"They don't all do it. Some of 'em leap until they get half a dozen elephants in line, then they stand off and watch the real artists finish the act. I can do that part of it now. But I tell you I'm going to be a leaper, Phil."

"Good for you! That's the way to talk. Keep out of trouble, work hard, don't talk too much, and you'll beat me yet," declared Phil. "And say!"

"What?"

"Be careful with that mule act tonight. You know Mr. Sparling will be in there watching you. It wouldn't take much more trouble to cause him to cut that act out of the programme, and then you might not be drawing so much salary. Fifty dollars a week is pretty nice for each of us. If we don't get swelled heads, but behave ourselves, we'll have a nice little pile of money by the time the season closes."

"Yes," agreed Teddy. "I guess that's so; but we'll be losing a lot of fun."

"I don't agree with you," laughed Phil.

The lads strolled into the menagerie tent on their way through to the dressing tent. The gasoline men were busy lighting their lamps and hauling them on center and quarter pole, while the menagerie attendants were turning the tongues of the cages about so that the horses could be hitched on promptly after the show in the big top began.

Some of the animals were munching hay, others of the caged beasts were lying with their noses poked through between the bars of their cages, blinking drowsily.

"I'd hate to be him," announced Teddy with a comprehensive wave of the hand as they passed the giraffe, which stood silent in his roped enclosure, his head far up in the shadows.

"Why?"

"For two reasons. Keeper tells me he can't make a sound. Doesn't bray, nor whinny, nor growl, nor bark, nor-- can't do anything. I'd rather be a lion or a tiger or something like that. If I couldn't do anything else, then, I could stand off and growl at folks."

Phil nodded and smiled.

"And what's your other reason for being glad you are not a giraffe?"

"Because--because--because when you had a sore throat think what a lot of neck you'd have to gargle!"

Phil laughed outright, and as the giraffe lowered its head and peered down into their faces, he thought, for the moment, that he could see the animal grin.

After this they continued on to the dressing tent, where they remained until time for the evening performance. This passed off without incident, Teddy and his mule doing nothing more sensational than kicking a rent in the ringmaster's coat.

After the show was over, and the tents had begun to come down, Phil announced his intention of going downtown for a lunch.

"This fresh air makes me hungry. You see, I am not used to it yet," he explained in an apologetic tone.

"You do not have to go down for a lunch, unless you want to," the bandmaster informed him.

"Why, is there a lunch place on the grounds?"

"No. We have an accommodation car on our section."

"What kind of car is that?"

"Lunch car. You can't get a heavy meal there, but you will find a nice satisfying lunch. The boss has it served at cost. He doesn't make any money out of the deal. You'll find it on our section."

"Good! Come along Teddy."

"Will I? That's where I'll spend my money," nodded Teddy, starting away at a jog trot.

"And your nights too, if they would let you," laughed Phil, following his companion at a more leisurely gait.

As they crossed the lot they passed "Red" Larry, as he had now been nicknamed by the showmen. Larry pretended not to see the boys, but there was an ugly scowl on his face that told Phil he did, and after the lads had gone on a piece Phil turned, casting a careless look back where the torches were flaring and men working and shouting.

"Red" Larry was not working now. He was facing the boys, shaking a clenched fist at them.

"I am afraid we haven't heard the last of our friend, Larry," said Phil.

"Who's afraid?" growled Teddy.

"Neither of us. But all the same we had better keep an eye on him while we are in his vicinity. We don't want to get into any more trouble--at least not, if we can possibly avoid it."

"Not till Mr. Sparling forgets about today? Is that it?"

"I guess it is," grinned Phil.

"He might take it seriously?"

"He already has done that. So be careful."

Teddy nodded. But the lads had not yet heard the last of "Red" Larry.

CHAPTER XII
THE HUMAN FOOTBALL

Ever try clowning, young man?" asked the Iron-Jawed Man.

Teddy Tucker shook his head.

"Why don't you?"

"Nobody ever asked me."

"Then you had better ask the boss to let you try it. Tell him you want to be a clown and that we will take you in and put you through your paces until you are able to go it alone."

The show had been on the road for nearly two weeks now, and every department was working like a piece of well-oiled machinery. The usual number of minor disasters had befallen the outfit during the first week, but now everything was system and method. The animals had become used to the constant moving, and to the crowds and the noise, so that their growls of complaint were few.

In that time Teddy and Phil had been going through their act on the flying rings daily, having shown great improvement since they closed with the show the previous fall. Their winter's work had proved of great benefit, and Mr. Sparling had complimented them several times lately.

Teddy was now devoting all his spare time to learning to somersault and do the leaping act from the springboard. He could, by this time, turn a somersault from the board, though his landing was less certain. Any part of his anatomy was liable to sustain the impact of his fall, but he fell in so many ludicrous positions that the other performers let it go at that, for it furnished them much amusement.

However, Teddy's unpopularity in the dressing tent had been apparent ever since he and the educated mule had made their sensational entry into that sacred domain, practically wrecking the place. Teddy and his pet had come near doing the same thing twice since, and the performers were beginning to believe there was method in Tucker's madness.

It had come to the point where the performers refused to remain in the dressing tent while Teddy and the mule were abroad, unless men with pike poles were stationed outside to ward off the educated mule when he came in from the ring. But Teddy didn't care. The lad was interested in the suggestion of the Iron-Jawed Man. Had he known that the suggestion had been made after secret conference of certain of the performers, Tucker might have felt differently about it. There was something in the air, but the Circus Boy did not know it.

"What kind of clown act would you advise me to get up?" he asked.

"Oh, you don't have to get it up. We'll do that for you. In fact, there is one act that most all clowns start with, and it will do as well as anything else for you. You see, you have to get used to being funny, or you'll forget yourself, and then you're of no further use as a clown."

"Yes, I know; but what is the act?"

"What do you say, fellows--don't you think the human football would fit him from the sawdust up?"

"Just the thing," answered the performers thus appealed to.

Mr. Miaco, the head clown, was bending over his trunk, his sides shaking with laughter, but Teddy did not happen to observe him, nor had he noticed that the head clown had had no part in the conversation.

"The human football?" questioned Teddy dubiously.

"Yes."

"What's that?"

"Oh, you dress up in funny makeup so you look like a huge ball."

"But what do I do after I have become a football?"

"Oh, you roll around in the arena, falling all over yourself and everybody who happens to get in your way; you bounce up and down and make all sorts of funny--"

"Oh, I know," cried Teddy enthusiastically. "I saw a fellow do that in a show once. He would fall on the ground on his back, then bounce up into the air several feet."

"You've hit it," replied a clown dryly.

"I remember how all the people laughed and shouted. I'll bet I'd make a hit doing that."

"You would!" shouted the performers in chorus.

The show was playing in Batavia, New York, on a rainy night, with rather a small house expected, so no better time could have been chosen for Teddy's first appearance as a clown.

"Had I better speak to Mr. Sparling about it?"

"Well, what do you think, fellows?"

"Oh, no, no! The old man won't care. If you make them laugh, he'll be tickled half to death."

"What do you say? Is it a go, Tucker?"

"Well, I'll think about it."

Teddy strolled out in the paddock, where he walked up and down a few times in the rain. But the more he thought about the proposition, the more enthusiastic he grew. He could see himself the center of attraction, and he could almost hear the howls of delight of the multitude.

"They'll be surprised. But I don't believe I had better go on without first speaking to Mr. Sparling. He might discharge me. He's had his eye on me ever since the mule tore up the dressing tent. But I won't tell Phil. I'll just give him a surprise. How he'll laugh when he sees me and finds out who I am."

Thus deciding, the lad ran through the tents out to the front door, where he asked for Mr. Sparling, knowing that by this time the owner's tent had been taken down and packed for shipment, even if it were not already under way on the flying squadron.

He learned that Mr. Sparling was somewhere in the menagerie tent. Hurrying back there, Teddy soon came upon the object of his search. At that moment he was standing in front of the cage of Wallace, the biggest lion in captivity, gazing at that shaggy beast thoughtfully.

"Mr. Sparling," called Teddy.

The showman turned, shooting a sharp glance at the flushed face of the Circus Boy.

"Well, what's wrong?"

"Nothing is wrong, sir."

"Come to kick about feed in the cook tent?"

"Oh, no, no, sir! Nothing like that. I've come to ask a favor of you."

"Humph! I thought as much. Well, what is it?"

"I--I think I'd like to be a clown, sir."

"A clown?" asked the showman, with elevated eyebrows.

"Yes, sir."

Mr. Sparling laughed heartily.

"Why, you're that already. You are a clown, though you may not know it. You've been a clown ever since you wore long dresses, I'll wager."

"But I want to be a real one," urged Teddy.

"What kind of clown?"

"I thought I'd like to be a human football." This time Mr. Sparling glanced at the boy in genuine surprise.

"A human football?"

"Yes, sir."

"What put that idea into your head?"

"Some of the fellows suggested it."

"Ah! I thought so," twinkled Mr. Sparling. "Who, may I ask?"

"Well, I guess most all of them did."

"I know, but who suggested it first?"

"I think the Iron-Jawed Man was the first to say that I ought to be a clown. He thought I would make a great hit."

"No doubt, no doubt," snapped the showman in a tone that led Teddy to believe he was angry about something.

"May I?"

Mr. Sparling reflected a moment, raised his eyes and gazed at the dripping roof of the menagerie tent.

"When is this first appearance to be made, if I may ask?"

"Oh, tonight. The fellows said it would be a good time, as there would not be a very big house."

"Oh, they did, eh? Well, go ahead. But remember you do it at your own risk."

"Thank you."

Teddy was off for the dressing room on a run.

"I'm It," he cried, bursting in upon them.

"Get the suit," commanded a voice. "He's It."

Somebody hurried to the property room, returning with a full rubber suit, helmet and all. As yet it was merely a bundle. They bade Teddy get into it, all hands crowding about him, offering suggestions and lending their assistance.

"My, I didn't know I was so popular here," thought the lad, pleased with these unusual attentions. "They must think I'm the real thing. I'll show them I am, too."

"Get the pump," directed the Iron-Jawed Man.

A bicycle pump was quickly produced, and, opening a valve, one of the performers began pumping air into the suit.

"Here, what are you doing?" demanded Teddy.

"Blowing you up--"

"Here, I don't want to be blown up."

"With a bicycle pump," added the performer, grinning through the powder and grease paint on his face.

"Say, you ought to use that on the press agent!"

The performers howled at this sally.

Teddy began to swell out of all proportion to his natural size, as the bicycle pump inflated his costume. In a few moments he had grown so large that he could not see his own feet, while the hood about his head left only a small portion of his face visible.

"Monster!" hissed a clown, shaking a fist in Teddy's face.

"I guess I am. I'd make a hit as the Fattest Boy on Earth in this rig, wouldn't I? I'll bet the Living Skeleton will be jealous when he sees me."

"There, I guess he's pumped up," announced the operator of the bicycle pump.

"Try it and see," suggested a voice.

"All right."

Teddy got a resounding blow that flattened him on the ground. But before he could raise his voice in protest he had bounded to his feet, and someone caught him, preventing his going right on over the other way.

The performers howled with delight.

"He'll do. He'll do," they shouted.

"Don't you do that again," warned the boy, a little dazed.

The time was at hand for the clowns to make their own grand entry.

"Come on, that's our cue!" shouted one, as the band struck up a new tune.

"I--I can't run. I'm too fat."

"We'll help you."

And they did. With a clown on either side of him, Teddy was rushed through the silk curtains and out past the bandstand, his feet scarcely touching the ground. Part of the time the clowns were half dragging him, and at other times carrying him.

At first the audience did not catch the significance of it. Straight for ring No. 1 Tucker's associates rushed him. But just as they reached the ring they let go of him.

Of course Teddy fell over the wooden ring curbing, and went rolling and bouncing into the center of the sawdust arena. Phil had made his change in the menagerie tent after finishing his elephant act, and was just entering the big top as Teddy made his sensational entrance. He caught sight of his companion at once.

"Who's that?" he asked of Mr. Sparling, who was standing at the entrance with a broad grin on his face.

"That, my dear Phil, is your very good friend, Mr. Teddy Tucker."

"Teddy? You don't mean it?"

"Yes; he has decided to be a clown, and I guess he is on the way. The people are kicking on the seats and howling."

"I should judge, from appearances, that the other clowns were getting even more entertainment out of his act than is the audience."

"It certainly looks that way. But let them go. It will do Master Teddy a whole lot of good."

A clown jumped to the ring curbing and made a speech about the wonderful human football, announcing at the same time that the championship game was about to be played.

Then they began to play in earnest. Some had slapsticks, others light barrel staves, and with these they began to belabor the human football, each blow being so loud that it could be heard all over the tent. Of course the blows did not hurt Teddy at all, but the bouncing and buffeting that he got aroused his anger.

One clown would pick the lad up and throw him to a companion, who, in turn, would drop him. Then the audience would yell with delight as the ball bounced to an upright position again. This the clowns kept up until Teddy did not know whether he were standing on his feet or his head. The perspiration was rolling down his face, getting into his eyes and blinding him.

"Quit it!" he howled.

"Maybe you'll ride the educated mule through the dressing tent again?" jeered a clown.

"Bring the mule out and let him knock the wind out of the rubber man!" suggested another.

"How do you like being a clown?"

This and other taunts were shouted at the rubber man, Teddy meanwhile expressing himself with unusual vehemence.

Mr. Sparling had in the meantime sent a message back to the paddock. He was holding his sides with laughter, while Phil himself was leaning against a quarter pole shouting with merriment.

Suddenly there came the sound of a clanging gong, interspersed with shouts from the far end of the tent.

The spectators quickly glanced in that direction, and they saw coming at a rapid rate the little patrol wagon drawn by four diminutive ponies, the outfit so familiar to the boys who attend the circus.

The clowns were surprised when they observed it, knowing that the patrol was not scheduled to enter at this time. Their surprise was even greater when the wagon dashed up and stopped where they were playing their game of football. Three mock policemen leaped out and rushed into the thick of the mock game.

As they did so they hurled the clowns right and left, standing some of them on their heads and beating them with their clubs, which, in this instance, proved to be slapsticks, that made a great racket.

This was a part of the act that the clowns had not arranged. It was a little joke that the owner of the show was playing on them. Quick to seize an opportunity to make a hit, Sparling had ordered out the show patrol, and the audience, catching the significance of it, shouted, swinging their hats and handkerchiefs.

The three policemen, after laying the clowns low, grabbed the helpless human football by the heels, dragging him to the wagon and dumping him in. They dropped the human football in so heavily that it bounced out again and hit the ground. The next time, as they threw Teddy in, one of the officers sat on him to

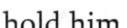

hold him.

The gong set up an excited clanging, and the ponies began racing around the arena the long way, and took the stretch to the paddock at a terrific speed, with the howls of the multitude sounding in their ears.

Reaching the dressing tent, the mock policemen let the air out of the rubber ball, whereat Teddy sat down heavily in a pail of water.

The performers danced around Tucker, singing an improvised song about the human football. Gradually the angry scowl on the face of the Circus Boy relaxed into a broad grin.

"How do you like being a clown now?" jeered the Iron-Jawed Man.

"Yes; how does it feel to be a football?" questioned another.

"I guess you got even with me that time," answered Teddy good-naturedly. "But say, that's easy compared with riding the educated mule."

CHAPTER XIII
DUCKED BY AN ELEPHANT

The great white billows of the Sparling Combined Shows were moving steadily across the continent. The receipts had exceeded Mr. Sparling's most sanguine expectations, and he was in great good humor.

Only one unpleasant incident had happened and that occurred at Franklin, Indiana. Phil and Teddy, while on their way to their car after the performance late at night, had been set upon by two men and quite severely beaten, though both lads had given a good account of themselves and finally driven off their assailants.

They did not report their experience to Mr. Sparling until the next morning, having gone directly to their car and put themselves to bed after having been fixed up with plasters and bandages by some of their companions. The next morning neither lad was particularly attractive to look at. However, bearing the taunts of the show people good-naturedly, they started for the cook tent just as they were in the habit of doing every day.

But Mr. Sparling had seen them as they passed his car on their way.

"Now, I wonder what those boys have been up to?" he scowled, watching their receding forms thoughtfully. "I'll find out."

And he did. He summoned the lads to his office in the tent soon after breakfast.

"I expected you would send for us," grinned Phil, as he walked in with Teddy.

"What about it? You are both sights!"

"Grease paint and powder will cover it up, I guess, Mr. Sparling."

"I'll hear how it happened."

"I can't tell you much about it," said Phil. "We were on our way to the car when a couple of men suddenly jumped out from a fence corner and went at us hammer and tongs. That's when we got these beauty spots. If we had seen the fellows coming we might not have been hit at all."

"Wait a minute; where did this occur?" demanded the showman.

"Just outside the lot at Franklin. It was very dark there, and, as you know, the sky was overcast."

"Did you know the men--had you ever seen them before?"

"I couldn't say as to that."

"No, sir; we couldn't say," added Teddy, nodding.

Mr. Sparling turned a cold eye upon Tucker.

"I haven't asked for remarks from you, young man. When I do you may answer."

Teddy subsided for the moment.

"But, had it been anyone you knew, you must have recognized their voices."

"They didn't say a word. Just pitched into us savagely. I think they might have done us serious injury had we not defended ourselves pretty well."

"It occurs to me that you were rather roughly handled as it was," said the showman, with a suspicion of a grin on his face. "Doctor fixed you up, I suppose?"

"Oh, no; it wasn't so bad as that."

"Have you any suspicion--do you think it was any of the show people?" demanded Mr. Sparling, eyeing Phil penetratingly.

"I don't know. Here is a button I got from the coat of one of the men. That may serve to identify him if he is one of our men. I haven't had a chance to look around this morning."

The showman quickly stretched forth his hand for the button, which he examined curiously.

"And here's a collar, too," chuckled Teddy.

"A collar? Where did you get that, young man?"

"Oh, I just yanked it off the other fellow. Guess it hasn't been to the laundry this season."

Mr. Sparling leaned back and laughed heartily.

"Between you, you boys will be the ruination of me. You take my mind off business so that I don't know what I'm about half of the time. But I can't get along without you. I'll look into this matter," he went on more gravely. "Tell the boss canvasman to send Larry and Bad Eye to me."

"Yes, sir."

The lads delivered the message.

Mr. Sparling's eyes twinkled as these two worthies sneaked into his tent, each with a hangdog expression on his face. "Red" Larry had a black eye, while Bad Eye's nose appeared to have listed to one side.

The showman glanced at Larry's coat, then at the button in his own hand. He nodded understandingly. Bad Eye was collarless.

"Here's a button that I think you lost off your coat last night, Larry," smiled Mr. Sparling sweetly. "And, Bad Eye, here's your collar. Better send it to the washer-woman."

The men were speechless for the moment.

"Go to the boss, both of you, and get your time. Then I want you to clear out of here."

"Wha--what--we ain't done nothing," protested Larry.

"And you had better not. If I see you about the circus lot again this season, I'll have you both in the nearest jail quicker than you can say 'scat!' Understand? Get out of here!"

The showman half rose from his chair, glaring angrily at them. His good-nature had suddenly left him, and the canvasmen, knowing what they might expect from the wrathful showman, stood not upon the order of their going. They ran.

Larry had left some of his belongings behind a cage in the menagerie tent, and he headed directly for that place to get it out and foot it for the village before Mr. Sparling should discover him on the grounds.

In going after his bundle Larry was obliged to pass the elephant station, where the elephants were taking their morning baths, throwing water over their backs from tubs that had been placed before them. A pail full of water had been left near old Emperor's tub by the keeper, because the tub would hold no more.

Emperor apparently had not observed it, nor did he seem to see the red-headed canvasman striding his way. Mr. Kennedy, the keeper, was at the far end of the line sweeping off the baby elephant with a broom, while Phil and Teddy were sitting on a pile of straw back of Emperor discussing their experience the previous evening.

"There's Red," said Teddy, pointing.

"Yes, and he seems to be in a great hurry about something. I'll bet Mr. Sparling

has discharged him. I'm sorry. I hate to see anybody lose his job, but I guess Red deserves it if anybody does. He's one of the fellows that attacked us last night. I haven't the least doubt about that."

"Yes, and he's got a button off his coat, too," added Teddy, peering around Emperor. "What I want now is to see a fellow with his collar torn off. I got a tent stake here by me that I'd like to meet him with."

"You would do nothing of the sort, Teddy Tucker! Hello, what's going on there?"

As Larry passed swiftly in front of Emperor, the old elephant's trunk suddenly wrapped itself about the pail of water unobserved by the discharged canvasman.

Emperor lifted the pail on high, quickly twisted it bottom side up and jammed it down over the head of Larry. The latter went down under the impact and before he could free himself from the pail and get up, Emperor had performed the same service for him with the tub of water.

Under the deluge Red Larry was yelling and choking, making desperate efforts to get up. He struggled free in a moment, and in his blind rage he hurled the empty pail full in Emperor's face, following it with a blow over the animal's trunk with a tent stake.

It was the elephant's turn to be angry now. He did not take into consideration that it was he that was to blame for the assault. Stretching out his trunk, he encircled the waist of the yelling canvasman, and, raising him on high, dashed him to the ground almost under his ponderous feet.

Phil had risen about the time the tub came down. At first he laughed; but when the elephant caught his victim, the lad knew that the situation was critical.

"Emperor! Down!" he shouted.

It was then that the elephant cast Red under his feet.

Phil darted forward just as a ponderous foot was raised to trample the man to death. Without the least sense of fear the lad ran in under Emperor, and, grabbing Larry by the heels, dragged him quickly out.

The elephant was furious at the loss of his prey, and, raising his trunk, trumpeted his disapproval, straining at his chains and showing every sign of dangerous restlessness.

After getting Larry out of harm's way, Phil sprang fearlessly toward his elephant friend.

"Quiet, Emperor, you naughty boy!" Forrest chided. "Don't you know you might have killed him? I wouldn't want anything to do with you if you had done a thing like that."

Gradually the great beast grew quiet and his sinuous trunk sought out the Circus Boy's pockets in search of sweets, of which there was a limited supply.

While this was going on Mr. Kennedy, the keeper, had hurried up and dashed a pail of water into the face of the now unconscious Larry. By this time Larry was well soaked down. He could not have been more so had he fallen in a mill pond. But the last bucketful brought him quickly to his senses.

"You--you'll pay for this," snarled Larry, shaking his fist at Phil Forrest.

"Why, I didn't do anything, Larry," answered the lad in amazement.

"You did. You set him on to me."

"That'll be about all from you, Mr. Red Head," warned Kennedy. "The kid didn't do anything but save your life. I wouldn't let a little thing like that trouble me if I were you. You've been doing something to that bull, or he'd never have used you like that. Why, Emperor is as gentle as a young kitten. He wouldn't hurt a fly unless the fly happened to bite him too hard. Phil, did you see that fellow do anything to him?"

Phil shook his head.

"Not now. He may have at some other time."

"That's it!"

Just then Mr. Sparling came charging down on the scene, having heard of the row out at the front door.

Larry saw him coming. He decided not to argue the question any further, but started on a run across the tent, followed by the showman, who pursued him with long, angry strides. But Larry ducked under the tent and got away before his pursuer could reach him, while Phil and Teddy stood holding their sides with laughter.

CHAPTER XIV
IN DIRE PERIL

Two days had passed and nothing more had been seen of the discharged canvasmen. Believing they were well rid of them all hands proceeded to forget about the very existence of Larry and Bad Eye.

As Phil was passing the roped-off enclosure where the elephants were tethered, the next morning just before the parade, he saw Mr. Kennedy regarding one of the elephants rather anxiously.

"What's the trouble? Anything gone wrong?" sang out the lad cheerily.

"Not yet," answered the keeper without turning his head.

"Something is bothering you or else you are planning out something new for the bulls," decided Phil promptly. "What is it?"

"I don't like the way Jupiter is acting."

"How?"

"He is ugly."

Phil ducked under the ropes and boldly walked over toward the swaying beast.

"Better keep away from him. He isn't to be trusted today."

"Going to send him out in the parade?"

"Haven't decided yet. I may think it best to leave Jupiter here with perhaps the baby elephant for company. He would cut up, I'm afraid, were I to leave him here alone. No; I think, upon second thought, that we had better take him out. It may take his mind from his troubles."

"What do you think is the matter with him?" questioned the Circus Boy, regarding the beast thoughtfully.

"That's what bothers me. He has never acted this way before. Usually there are some signs that I told you about once before that tells one an elephant is going bad."

"You mean the tear drops that come out from the slit under the eye?"

"Yes. There has been nothing of that sort with Jupiter."

"He acts to me as if he had a bad stomach," suggested Phil wisely.

"That's right. That expresses it exactly. I guess we'll have to give him a pill to set him straight. But Jupiter never was much of a hand for pills. He'll object if we suggest it."

"Then don't suggest it. Just give it to him in his food."

"You can't fool him," answered Mr. Kennedy, with a shake of the head. "He'd smell it a rod away, and that would make him madder than ever. The best way is to make him open his mouth and throw the pill back as far as possible in his throat."

"Have you told Mr. Sparling?"

"No. He doesn't like to be bothered with these little things. He leaves that all to me. It's a guess, though, as to just what to do under these conditions. No two cases, any more than any two elephants, are alike when it comes to disposition and treatment."

"No; I suppose not."

"Where are you going now, Phil?"

"Going back to the dressing tent to get ready for the parade. Hope you do not have any trouble."

"No; I guess I shan't. I can manage to hold him, and if I don't, I'll turn Emperor loose. He makes a first-rate policeman."

Phil hurried on to the dressing tent, for he was a little late this morning, for which he was not wholly to blame, considerable time having been lost in his interview with Mr. Sparling.

In the hurry of preparation for the parade, Phil forgot all about Mr. Kennedy's concern over Jupiter. But he was reminded of it again when he rode out to fall in line with the procession. Mr. Kennedy and his charges, all well in hand, were just emerging from the menagerie tent to take their places for the parade. Jupiter was among them. He saw, too, that Mr. Kennedy was walking by Jupiter's side, giving him almost his exclusive attention.

Phil's place in the parade this season was with a body of German cavalry. He wore a plumed hat, with a gaudy uniform and rode a handsome bay horse, one of the animals used in the running race at the close of the circus. Phil had become

very proficient on horseback and occasionally had entered the ring races, being light enough for the purpose. He had also kept up his bareback practice, under the instruction of Dimples, until he felt quite proud of his achievements.

Vincennes, where the show was to exhibit that day, was a large town, and thousands of people had turned out to view the parade which had been extensively advertised as one of the greatest features ever offered to the public.

"They seem to like it," grinned Phil, turning to the rider beside him.

"Act as if they'd never seen a circus parade before," answered the man. "But wait till we get out in some of the way-back towns in the West."

"I thought we were West now?"

"Not until we get the other side of the Mississippi, we won't be. They don't call Indiana West. We'll be getting there pretty soon, too. According to the route card, we are going to make some pretty long jumps from this on."

"We do not go to Chicago, do we?"

"No. Show's not quite big enough for that town. We go south of it, playing some stands in Illinois, then striking straight west. Hello, what's the row up ahead there?"

"What row, I didn't see anything."

"Something is going on up there. See! The line is breaking!"

The part of the parade in which Phil was located was well up toward the elephants, the animals at that moment having turned a corner, moving at right angles to Phil's course.

"It's the elephants!" cried the lad aghast.

"What's happening?"

"They have broken the line!"

All was confusion at the point on which the two showmen had focused their eyes.

"It's a stampede, I do believe!" exclaimed Phil. "I wonder where Mr. Kennedy is? I don't see him anywhere."

"There! They're coming this way."

"What, the elephants? Yes, that's so. Oh, I'm afraid somebody will be killed."

"If there hasn't already been," growled Phil's companion. "I'm going to get out of this while I have the chance. I've seen elephants on the rampage before." Saying which, the showman turned his horse and rode out of the line. His example was followed by many of the others.

People were screaming and rushing here and there, horses neighing, and the animals in the closed cages roaring in a most terrifying way.

Phil pulled his horse up short, undecided what to do. He had never seen a stampede before, but desperate as the situation seemed, he felt no fear.

The elephants, with lowered heads, were charging straight ahead. Now Phil saw that which seemed to send his heart right up into his throat.

Little Dimples had been riding in a gayly bedecked two-wheeled cart, drawn by a prancing white horse. Dressed in white from head to foot, she looked the dainty creature that she was.

Dimples, seeing what had happened, had wheeled her horse quickly out of line, intending to turn about and drive back along the line. It would be a race between the white horse and the elephants, but she felt sure she would be able to make it and turn down a side street before the stampeding herd reached her.

She might have done so, had it not been for one unforeseen incident. As she dashed along a rider, losing his presence of mind, if indeed, he had had any to lose, drove his horse directly in front of her. The result was a quick collision, two struggling horses lying kicking in the dust of the street, and a white-robed figure lying stretched out perilously near the flying hoofs.

The force of the collision had thrown Little Dimples headlong from her seat in the two wheeled cart, and there she lay, half-dazed with the herd of elephants thundering down upon her.

Phil took in her peril in one swift glance.

"She'll be killed! She'll be killed!" he cried, all the color suddenly leaving his face.

All at once he drove the rowels of his spurs against the sides of his mount. The animal sprang away straight toward the oncoming herd, but Phil had to fight every inch of the way to keep the horse from turning about and rushing back, away from the peril that lay before it.

The lad feared he would not be able to reach Dimples in time, but with frequent prods of spur and crop, uttering little encouraging shouts to the frightened horse, he dashed on, dodging fleeing showmen and runaway horses at almost every jump.

He forged up beside the girl at a terrific pace. But, now that he was there, the lad did not dare dismount, knowing that were he to do so, his horse would quickly break away from him, thus leaving them both to be crushed under the feet of the ponderous beasts.

It was plain to Phil that Jupiter must have gone suddenly bad, and, starting on a stampede, had carried the other bulls with him. And he even found himself wondering if anything had happened to his friend Kennedy, the elephant trainer. If Kennedy were on his feet he would be after them.

As it was, no one appeared to be chasing the runaway beasts.

Phil leaned far from the saddle grasping the woman by her flimsy clothing. It gave way just as he had begun to lift her, intending to pull her up beside him on the horse's back.

Twice he essayed the feat, each time with the same result. The bay was dancing further away each time, and the elephants were getting nearer. The uproar was deafening, which, with the trumpetings of the frightened elephants, made the stoutest hearts quail.

With a grim determination Forrest once more charged alongside of Dimples. As he did so she opened her eyes, though Phil did not observe this, else he might have acted differently.

As it was he threw himself from the bay while that animal was still on the jump. Keeping tight hold of the saddle pommel, the reins bunched in the hand that grasped it, Phil dropped down. When he came up, Dimples was on his arm.

He then saw that she was herself again.

"Can you hold on if I get you up?"

"Yes. You're a good boy."

Phil made no reply, but, with a supreme effort, threw the girl into the saddle. To do so he was obliged to let go the pommel and the reins for one brief instant. But he succeeded in throwing Dimples up to the saddle safely, where she quickly secured herself.

The bay was off like a shot, leaving Phil directly in front of the oncoming elephants.

"Run! I'll come back and get you," shouted Dimples over her shoulder.

"You can't. The reins are over the bay's head," he answered.

She was powerless to help. Dimples realized this at once. She was in no danger herself. She was such a skillful rider that it made little difference whether the reins were in her hand or on the ground, so far as maintaining her seat was concerned. With Phil, however, it was different.

"I guess I might as well stand still and take it," muttered the lad grimly.

He turned, facing the mad herd, a slender but heroic figure in that moment of peril.

CHAPTER XV
EMPEROR TO THE RESCUE

Get back!" shouted the boy.

He had descried Teddy Tucker driving his own mount toward him. Teddy was coming to the rescue in the face of almost certain death.

"You can't make it! Go back!"

Whether or not Teddy heard and understood, did not matter, for at that moment the view of the plucky lad was shut off by the elephants forming their charging line into crescent shape.

"Emperor!" he called in a shrill penetrating voice. But in the dust of the charge he could not make out which one was Emperor, yet he continued calling lustily.

"Emperor!"

Phil threw his hands above his head as was his wont when desirous of having the old elephant pick him up.

Right across the center of the crescent careened a great hulking figure, uttering loud trumpetings--trumpetings that were taken up by his companions until the very ground seemed to shake.

Phil's back was half toward the big elephant, and in the noise he did not distinguish a familiar note in the call.

All at once he felt himself violently jerked from the ground. The lad was certain that his time had come. But out of that cloud of dust, in which those who looked, believed that the little Circus Boy had gone down to his death, Phil Forrest rose right up into the air and was dropped unharmed to the back of old Emperor.

For the moment he was so dizzy that he was unable to make up his mind what had happened or where he was. Then it all came to him. He was on Emperor's back.

"Hurrah!" shouted Phil. "Good old Emperor! Steady, steady, Emperor! That's a good fellow."

He patted the beast's head with the flat of his hand, crooned to him, using every artifice that he knew to quiet the nerves of his big friend.

Little by little Emperor appeared to come out of his fright, until the lad felt almost certain that the big beast would take orders. He tried the experiment.

"Left, Emperor!"

The elephant swerved sharply to the left, aided by a sharp tap of the riding crop which Phil still carried.

Phil uttered a little cry of exultation.

"Now, if I can head them off!"

With this in mind he gradually worked Emperor around until the herd had been led into a narrow street. Here, Phil began forcing his mount back and forth across the street in an effort to check the rush of the stampede, all the time calling out the command to slow down, which he had learned from Mr. Kennedy.

He was more successful than he had even dreamed he could be.

"Now, if I am not mistaken, that street beyond there leads out to the lot. I'll see if I can make them go that way."

All did save Jupiter, who charged straight ahead for some distance, then turning sharply tore back and joined his fellows.

"If I had a hook I believe I could lead him. He's a very bad elephant. I hope nobody has been killed."

It was more quiet in the street where Forrest now found himself, and by degrees the excitement that had taken possession of the huge beasts began to wear off.

Phil uttered his commands to them in short, confident tones, all the time drawing nearer and nearer to the circus lot.

Very soon the fluttering flags from the big top were seen above the intervening housetops.

"I'm going to win--oh, I hope I do!" breathed the Circus Boy.

With rapid strides, at times merging into a full run, the beasts tore along, now understanding that they were nearing their quarters, where safety and quiet would be assured.

And, beyond that, it was time for their dinners. Already bales of hay had been placed in front of their quarters, and the elephants knew it.

As the procession burst into the circus lot a dozen attendants started on a run toward them.

"Keep off!" shouted Phil. "Do you want to stampede them again? Keep away, I tell you and I'll get them home. Drive all the people out of the way in case the bulls make another break. That's all you can do now."

Now young Forrest urged Emperor to the head of the line of bobbing beasts, feeling sure that the others would follow him in now.

They did. The whole line of elephants swept in through the opening that the attendants had quickly made by letting down a section of the side walls of the menagerie tent, with Phil Forrest a proud and happy boy, perched on the head of old Emperor.

"Halt!"

He went at it with all the confidence and skill of a professional elephant trainer.

"Stations!"

Each beast walked to his regular place, a dozen sinuous trunks gathering up as many wisps of hay.

"Back up! Back, Jupiter!"

As docile as if they never had left the tent, each huge beast slowly felt his way into his corner.

"Good boy, Emperor!" glowed Phil holding out a small bag of peanuts, which Emperor quickly stowed away in his mouth bag and all.

"You greedy fellow! Now get back into your own corner!"

The elephant did so.

"You fellows keep away from here," warned Phil as the anxious tent men began crowding around him. "Don't let anybody get these big fellows excited. We've had trouble enough for one day."

Phil then began chaining down the beasts, his first care being to secure the unruly Jupiter. But Jupiter's fit of bad temper seemed to have left him entirely. He was as peaceful as could be, and, to show that he was good, he showered a lot of hay all over Phil.

"You bad, bad boy!" chided the lad. "All this is just because you let your temper get the best of you. I think perhaps Mr. Sparling may have something to say to you if anyone has been killed or seriously hurt. Oh, you want some peanuts, do you? I haven't any, but I'll get you some, though goodness knows you don't deserve any. Bring me some peanuts, will you please?"

An attendant came running with a bag of them. Phil met him halfway, not wishing the man to approach too near. With the bag in his hand the boy walked slowly down the line, giving to each of his charges a small handful.

This was the final act in subduing them. They were all thoroughly at home and perfectly contented now, and Phil had chained the last one down, except the baby elephant, that usually was left free to do as it pleased, providing it did not get too playful.

At this moment Phil heard a great shouting out on the lot.

"Go out there and stop that noise!" the boy commanded. He was as much in charge of the show at that moment as if he had been the proprietor himself.

Shortly after that Mr. Kennedy came rushing in on one of the circus ponies that he had taken from a parade rider. Phil was delighted to see that the keeper was uninjured.

"Did you do this, Phil Forrest?" he shouted bursting in.

"Yes. But I'll have to do it all over again if you keep on yelling like that. What happened to you?"

"Jupiter threw me over a fence, into an excavation where they were digging for a new building. I thought I was dead, but after a little I came to and crawled out. It was all over but the shouting then."

"Did you know I had them?"

"No; not until I got near the lot. I followed their tracks you see. Finally some people told me a kid was leading the herd back here. I knew that was you. Phil Forrest, you are a dandy. I can't talk now! I'm too winded. I'll tell you later on what I think of your kind. Now I'm going to whale the daylights out of that Jupiter."

"Please don't do anything of the sort," begged Phil. "He is quiet now. He has forgotten all about it. I am afraid if you try to punish him you will only make him worse."

"Good elephant sense," emphasized the keeper. "You ought to be on the animals."

"It seems to me that I have been pretty well on them today," grinned the lad. "Oh, was anybody killed?"

"I think not. Don't believe anyone was very seriously hurt. You see, that open lot there gave the people plenty of chance to see what was coming. They had plenty of time to get away after that."

"I'm so glad. I hope no one was killed."

"Reckon there would have been if you hadn't got busy when you did."

"Have you seen Mrs. Robinson? I'm rather anxious about her."

"There she is now."

Dimples had changed her torn white dress for a short riding skirt, and when Phil turned about she was running toward him with outstretched arms. He braced himself and blushed violently.

"Oh, you dear," cried the impulsive little equestrienne, throwing both arms about Phil's neck. "I wish my boy could have seen you do that! It was splendid. You're a hero! You'll see what a craze the people will make of you--"

"I--I think they are more likely to chase us out of town," laughed Phil. "We must have smashed up things pretty thoroughly downtown."

"Never mind; Mr. Sparling will settle the damage. The only trouble will be that he won't have anyone to scold. You saved the day, Phil, and you saved me as well. Of course I'm not much, but I value my precious little life just as highly as the next one--I mean the next person."

"The bay ran away with you, didn't he?"

"I suppose that's what some people would call it. It would have been a glorious ride if it hadn't been that I expected you were being trampled to death back there. The bay brought me right to the lot, then stopped, of course. Circus horses have a lot of sense. I heard right away that you were not injured and that you were bringing the bulls in. Then I was happy. I'm happy now. We'll have a lesson after the show. You--"

"When do you think I shall be fit to go in the ring?"

"Fit now! You're ahead of a good many who have been working at it for years, and I mean just what I'm saying. There is Mr. Sparling. Come on; run along back to the paddock with me. I haven't finished talking with you yet."

"Perhaps he may want me," hesitated Phil.

"Nothing very particular. He'll want to have it out with Mr. Kennedy first. Then, if he wants you, he can go back and hunt you up, or send for you. Mr. Sparling knows how to send for people when he wants them, doesn't he?" twinkled Dimples.

"I should say he did," grinned Phil. "He's not bashful. Has my friend Teddy got back yet?"

"Haven't seen him. Why? Worried about him?"

"Not particularly. He has a habit of taking care of himself under most circumstances."

Dimples laughed heartily.

"It will take more than a stampede to upset him. He'll make a showman if he ever settles down to the work in earnest."

"He has settled down, Mrs. Robinson," answered Phil with some dignity.

"My, my! But you needn't growl about it. I was paying him a compliment."

Thus she chattered on until they reached the paddock. They had been there but a few moments before the expected summons for Phil was brought.

CHAPTER XVI
AN UNEXPECTED PROMOTION

Phil responded rather reluctantly. He would have much preferred to sit out in the paddock talking circus with Little Dimples.

He found Mr. Sparling striding up and down in front of the elephant enclosure.

"I hope nothing very serious happened, Mr. Sparling," greeted Phil, approaching him.

"If you mean damages, no. A few people knocked down, mostly due to their own carelessness. I've got the claim-adjuster at work settling with all we can get hold of. But we'll get it all back tonight, my boy. We'll have a turn-away this afternoon, too, unless I am greatly mistaken. Why, they're lining up outside the front door now."

"I'm glad for both these things," smiled Phil. "Especially so because no one was killed."

"No. But one of our bareback riders was put out of business for a time."

"Is that so? Who?"

"Monsieur Liebman."

"Oh, that's too bad. What happened to him?"

"Someone ran him down. He was thrown and sprained his ankle. He won't ride for sometime, I reckon. But come over here and sit down. I want to have a little chat with you."

Mr. Sparling crossed the tent, sitting down on a bale of straw just back of the monkey cage. The simians were chattering loudly, as if discussing the exciting incidents of the morning. But as soon as they saw the showman they flocked to the back of the cage, hanging by the bars, watching him to find out what he was going to do.

He made a place for Phil beside him.

"Sit down."

"Thank you."

"I was just running up in my mind, on my way back, that, in actual figures, you've saved me about ten thousand dollars. Perhaps it might be double that. But that's near enough for all practical purposes."

"I saved you--" marveled Phil, flushing.

"Yes."

"How?"

"Well, you began last year, and you have started off at the same old pace this season. Today you have gone and done it again. That was one of the nerviest things I ever saw. I wouldn't have given a copper cent for your life, and I'll bet you wouldn't, either."

"N-o-o," reflected Phil slowly, "I thought I was a goner."

"While the rest of our crowd were hiking for cover, like a lot of 'cold feet,' you were diving right into the heart of the trouble, picking up my principal equestrienne. Then you sent her away and stopped to face the herd of bulls. Jumping giraffes, but it was a sight!"

By this time the monkeys had gone back to finish their animated discussion.

"I do not deserve any credit for that. I was caught and I thought I might as well face the music."

"Bosh! I heard you calling for Emperor, and I knew right away that that little head of yours was working like the wheels of a chariot in a Roman race. I knew what you were trying to do, but I'd have bet a thousand yards of canvas you never would. You did, though," and the showman sighed.

Phil was very much embarrassed and sat kicking his heels into the soft turf, wishing that Mr. Sparling would talk about something else.

"The whole town is talking about it. I'm going to have the press agent wire the story on ahead. I told him, just before I came in, that if he'd follow you he'd get 'copy' enough to last him all the rest of his natural life. All that crowd out there has come because there was a young circus boy with the show, who had a head on his shoulders and the pluck to back his gray matter."

"Have you talked with Mr. Kennedy?" asked Phil, wishing to change the personal trend of the conversation.

"Yes; why?"

"Did he say what he thought was the matter with Jupiter?"

"He didn't know. He knew only that Jupiter had been 'off' for nearly two days. Kennedy said something about a bad stomach. Why do you ask that question?" demanded the showman, with a shrewd glance at the boy.

"Because I have been wondering about Jupiter quite a little since morning. I've been thinking, Mr. Sparling."

"Now what are you driving at? You've got something in your head. Out with it!"

"It may sound foolish, but--"

"But what?"

"While Jupiter was bad, he showed none of the signs that come from a fit of purely bad temper--that is, before the stampede."

"That's right."

"Then what brought it on?" asked Phil looking Mr. Sparling squarely in the eyes.

For a few seconds man and boy looked at each other without a word.

"What's your idea?" asked the showman quietly.

"It's my opinion that somebody doctored him--gave him something--"

The showman uttered a long, low whistle.

"You've hit it! You've hit it!" he exclaimed, bringing a hand down on the lad's knee with such force that Phil winced. "It's one of those rascally canvasmen that I discharged. Oh, if ever I get my hands on him it will be a sorry day for him! You haven't seen him about, have you?"

"I thought I caught a glimpse of him on the street yesterday during the parade, but he disappeared so quickly that I could not be sure."

Mr. Sparling nodded reflectively.

"You probably heard how Emperor ducked him and--"

"Yes; you remember I came up just after the occurrence. I'll tell you what I want you to do."

"Yes?"

"I'll release you from the parade for tomorrow, and perhaps longer, and I want you to spend your time moving around among the downtown crowds to see if you can spot him. If you succeed, well you will know what to do."

"Want me to act as a sort of detective?" grinned Phil.

"Well, you might put it that way, but I don't. You are serving me if--"

"Yes; I know that. I am glad to serve you in any way I can."

"I don't have to take your word for that," laughed Mr. Sparling. "I think you have shown me. I have been thinking of another matter. It has been in my mind for several days."

Phil glanced up inquiringly.

"How would you like to come out front?"

"You mean?"

"To join my staff? I need someone just like you--a young man with ideas, with the force to put them into execution after he has developed them. You are the one I want."

"But, Mr. Sparling--"

"Wait till I get through. You can continue with your acts if you wish, just the same, and give your odd moments to me."

"In what capacity?"

"Well, for the want of a better name we'll call it a sort of confidential man."

"I appreciate the offer more than I can tell you, Mr. Sparling. But--but--"

"But what?"

"I want to go through the mill in the ring. I want to learn to do everything that almost anyone can do there."

The showman laughed.

"Then you would be able to do what few men ever have succeeded in doing. You would be a wonder. I'm not saying that you are not that already, in your way. But you would be a wonder among showmen."

"I can do quite a lot of things now."

"I know you can. And you will. What do you say?"

"It's funny, but since you told me of the accident to your bareback man, I was going to ask you something."

"What?"

"Rather, I was going to suggest--"

"Well, out with it!"

"I was going to suggest that you let me fill in his place until he is able to work again. It would save you the expense of getting a new performer on, and would hold the job for the present man."

"You, a bareback rider?"

Phil nodded.

"But you can't ride!"

"But I can," smiled the lad. "I've been at it almost ever since we started the season. I've been working every day."

"Alone?"

"No. Mrs. Robinson has been teaching me. Of course, I am not much of a rider, but I can manage to stick on somehow."

The manager was regarding him thoughtfully.

"As I have intimated strongly before this, you beat anything I ever have seen in all my circus experience. You say you can ride bareback?"

"Yes."

"I should like to see what you can do. Mind you, I'm not saying I'll let you try it in public. Just curious, you know, to see what you have been doing."

"Now--will you see me ride now?"

Mr. Sparling nodded.

"Then I'll run back and get ready. I'll be out in a few minutes," laughed the boy, as, with sparkling eyes and flushed face, he dashed back to the dressing tent to convey the good news to Little Dimples.

"I knew it," she cried enthusiastically. "I knew you would be a rival soon. Now I've got to look out or I shall be out of a job in no time. Hurry up and get your working clothes on. I'll have the gray out by the time you are ready."

Twenty minutes later Phil Forrest presented himself in the ring, with Little Dimples following, leading the old gray ring horse.

"Come up to ring No. 2," directed the owner. "They haven't leveled No. 1 down yet. How's this? Don't you use the back pad to ride on?" questioned Mr. Sparling in a surprised tone.

"No, sir. I haven't used the pad at all yet."

"Very well; I'm ready to see you fall off."

Phil sprang lightly to the back of the ring horse while Dimples, who had brought a ringmaster's whip with her, cracked the whip and called shrilly to her horse. The old gray fell into its accustomed easy gallop, Phil sitting lightly on the animal's hip, moving up and down with the easy grace of a finished rider.

After they had swept twice around the ring, the boy sprang to his feet, facing ahead, and holding his short crop in both hands, leaning slightly toward the center of the ring, treading on fairy feet from one end of the broad back to the other.

Next he varied his performance by standing on one foot, holding the other up by one hand, doing the same graceful step that he had on both feet a moment before.

Now he tried the same feats riding backwards, a most difficult performance for any save a rider of long experience.

Mrs. Robinson became so absorbed in his riding that she forgot to urge the gray along or to crack the whip. The result was that the old horse stopped suddenly.

Phil went right on. He was in a fair way to break his neck, as he was plunging toward the turf head first.

"Ball!" she cried, meaning to double oneself up into as near an approach to a round ball as was possible.

But Phil already had begun to do this very thing. And he did another remarkable feat at the same time. He turned his body in the air so that he faced to the front, and the next instant landed lightly on his feet outside the ring.

Phil blew a kiss to the amazed owner, turning back to the ring again.

By this time Mrs. Robinson had placed the jumping board in the ring--a short piece of board, one end of which was built up about a foot from the ground. Then she started the ring horse galloping again.

Phil, measuring his distance, took a running start and vaulted, landing on his feet on the animal's back, then, urging his mount on to a lively gallop about the sawdust ring, he threw himself into a whirlwind of graceful contortions and rapid movements, adding some of his own invention to those usually practiced by bareback riders.

Phil dropped to the hip of the gray, his face flushed with triumph, his eyes sparkling.

"How is it, Mr. Sparling?" he called.

The showman was clapping his hands and clambering down the aisle from his position near the top row of seats.

"You don't mean to tell me you have never tried bareback riding before this season?" he demanded.

"No, sir; this is my first experience."

"Then all I have to say is that you will make one of the finest bareback riders in the world if you keep on. It is marvelous, marvelous!"

"Thank you," glowed the lad. "But if there is any credit coming to anyone it is due to Mrs. Robinson. She taught me how to do it," answered Phil gallantly.

Little Dimples shook a small, brown fist at him.

"He knows how to turn a pretty compliment as well as he knows how to ride, Mr. Sparling," bubbled Dimples. "You should just hear the nice things he said to me back in the paddock," she teased.

Phil blushed furiously.

"Shall I ride again?" he asked.

"Not necessary," answered the owner. "But, by the way, you might get up and do a somersault. Do a backward turn with the horse at a gallop," suggested Mr. Sparling, with a suspicion of a smile at the corners of his mouth.

"A somersault?" stammered Phil, somewhat taken back. "Why--I-- I--I guess I couldn't do that; I haven't learned to do that yet."

"Not learned to do it? I am surprised."

Phil looked crestfallen.

"I am surprised, indeed, that there is one thing in this show that you are unable to do." The manager broke out into a roar of laughter, in which Little Dimples joined merrily.

"May I go on?" asked the lad somewhat apprehensively.

"May you? May you? Why, I--"

At that moment Teddy Tucker came strolling lazily in with a long, white feather tucked in the corner of his mouth.

The showman's eyes were upon it instantly.

"What have you there?" he demanded.

"Feather," answered Teddy thickly.

"I see it. Where did you get it?"

"Pulled it out of the pelican's tail. Going to make a pen of it to use when I write to the folks at Edmeston," answered the boy carelessly.

"You young rascal!" thundered Mr. Sparling. "What do you mean by destroying my property like that? I'll fine you! I'll teach you!"

"Oh, it didn't hurt the pelican any. Besides, he's got more tail than he can use in his business, anyway."

"Get out of here!" thundered the manager in well-feigned anger. "I'll forget myself and discharge you first thing you know. What do you want?"

"I was going to ask you something," answered Teddy slowly.

"You needn't. You needn't. It won't do you any good. What is it you were going to ask me?"

"I was going to ask you if I might go in the leaping act."

"The leaping act?"

"Yes, sir. The one where the fellows jump over the elephants and--"

"Ho, ho, ho! What do you think of that, Phil? What do you--"

"I can do it. You needn't laugh. I've done it every day for three weeks. I can jump over four elephants and maybe five, now. I can--"

"Yes, I have seen him do it, Mr. Sparling," vouched Phil. "He is going to make a very fine leaper."

The showman removed his broad sombrero, wiped the perspiration from his brow, glancing from one to the other of the Circus Boys.

"May I?"

"Yes, yes. Go ahead. Do anything you want to. I'm only the hired man around here anyhow," snapped the showman, jamming his hat down over his head and striding away, followed by the merry laughter of Little Dimples.

CHAPTER XVII
THE CIRCUS BOYS WIN NEW LAURELS

Bareback riders out!" shouted the callboy, poking his head into the dressing tent.

"Get out!" roared a clown, hurling a fellow performer's bath brush at the boy, which the youngster promptly shied back at the clown's head, then prudently made his escape to call Little Dimples in the women's dressing tent.

Phil Forrest, proud and happy, bounded out into the paddock, resplendent in pink tights, a black girdle about his loins, sparkling with silver spangles.

Little Dimples ran out at about the same time.

"How do I look?" he questioned, his face wreathed in smiles.

"If you ride half as well as you look today, you will make the hit of your life," twinkled Dimples merrily. "There, don't blush. Run along. The band is playing our entrance tune. Mr. Ducro will be in a fine temper if we are a second behind time."

For that day, and until Phil could break in on another animal, Little Dimples had loaned her gray to him, for Phil did not dare to try the experiment of riding a new horse at his first appearance. Altogether too much depended upon his first public exhibition as a bareback rider to permit his taking any such chances.

Dimples owned two horses, so she rode the second one this day.

As Phil walked lightly the length of the big top, which he was obliged to do to reach ring No. 1 in which he was to ride, his figure, graceful as it was, appeared almost fragile. He attracted attention because of this fact alone, for the people did not recognize in him the lad who had that morning stayed the stampede of the herd of huge elephants.

"Now keep cool. Don't get excited," warned Dimples as she left him to enter the ring where she was to perform. "Forget all about those people out there, and they will do the rest."

Phil nodded and passed on smiling. Reaching his ring he quickly kicked off his pumps and leaped lightly to the back of his mount, where he sat easily while the gray slowly walked about the sawdust arena.

"Ladies and gentlemen," announced the equestrian director. "You see before you the hero of the day, the young man who, unaided, stopped the charge of a herd of great elephants, saving, perhaps many lives besides doing a great service for the Sparling Combined Shows."

"What did you do that for?" demanded Phil, squirming uneasily on the slippery seat where he was perched.

"Unfortunately," continued the Director, "our principal male bareback rider was slightly injured in that same stampede. The management would not permit him to appear this evening on that account, for the Sparling Combined Shows believe in treating its people right. Our young friend here has consented to ride in the regular rider's place. It is his first appearance in any ring as a bareback rider. I might add that he has been practicing something less than three weeks for this act; therefore any slips that he may make you will understand. Ladies and gentlemen, I take pleasure in introducing to you Master Phillip Forrest, the hero of the day--a young man who is winning new laurels on the tanbark six days in every week!"

The audience, now worked up to the proper pitch of enthusiasm by the words of the director, howled its approval, the spectators drumming on the seats with their feet and shouting lustily. Phil had not had such an ovation since the day he first rode Emperor into the ring when he joined the circus in Edmeston.

The lad's face was a few shades deeper pink than his tights, and nervous excitement seemed to suddenly take possession of him.

"I wish you hadn't done that," he laughed. "I'll bet I fall off now, for that."

"Tweetle! Tweetle!" sang the whistle.

Crash!

At a wave of the bandmaster's baton, the band suddenly launched into a smashing air.

The ringmaster's whip cracked with an explosive sound, at which the gray mare, unaffected by the noise and the excitement, started away at a measured gallop, her head rising and falling like the prow of a ship buffeting a heavy sea.

Phil was plainly nervous. He knew it. He felt that he was going to make an unpleasant exhibition of himself.

"Get up! Get going! Going to sit there all day?" questioned the ringmaster.

Phil threw himself to his feet. Somehow he missed his footing in his nervousness, and the next instant he felt himself falling.

"There, I've done it!" groaned the lad, as he dropped lightly on all fours well outside the wooden ring curbing, which he took care to clear in his descent.

"Oh, you Rube! You've gone and done it now," growled the ringmaster. "It's all up. You've lost them sure."

The audience was laughing and cheering at the same time.

Feeling her rider leave her back the gray dropped her gallop and fell into a slow trot.

Phil scrambled to his feet very red in the face, while Mr. Sparling, from the side lines, stood leaning against a quarter pole with a set grin on his face. His confidence in his little Circus Boy was not wholly lost yet.

"Keep her up! Keep her up! What ails you?" snapped Phil.

All the grit in the lad's slender body seemed to come to the front now. His eyes were flashing and he gripped the little riding whip as if he would vent his anger upon it.

The ringmaster's whip had exploded again and the gray began to gallop. Phil paused on the ring curbing with head slightly inclined forward, watching the gray with keen eyes.

Phil had forgotten that sea of human faces out there now. He saw only that broad gray, rosined back that he must reach and cling to, but without a slip this time.

All at once he left the curbing, dashing almost savagely at his mount.

"He'll never make it from the ground," groaned Mr. Sparling, realizing that Phil had no step to aid him in his effort to reach the back of the animal.

The lad launched himself into the air as if propelled by a spring. He landed fairly on the back of the ring horse, wavered for one breathless second, then fell into the pose of the accomplished rider.

"Y-i-i-i--p! Y-i-i-i-p!" sang the shrill voice of Little Dimples far down in ring No. 1.

"Y-i-i-i-p!" answered the Circus Boy, while the spectators broke into thunders of applause.

Mr. Sparling, hardened showman that he was, brushed a suspicious hand across his eyes and sat down suddenly.

"Such grit, Such grit!" he muttered.

Phil threw himself wildly into his work, taking every conceivable position known to the equestrian world, and essaying many daring feats that he had never tried before. It seemed simply impossible for the boy to fall, so sure was his footing. Now he would spring from the broad back of the gray, and run across the ring, doing a lively handspring, then once more vault into a standing position on the mare.

Suddenly the band stopped playing, for the rest that is always given the performers. But Phil did not pause.

"Keep her up!" Forrest shouted, bringing down his whip on the flanks of his mount and, in a fervor of excitement and stubborn determination, going at his work like a whirlwind.

Mr. Sparling, catching the spirit of the moment scrambled to his feet and rushed to the foot of the bandstand, near which he had been sitting.

"Play, you idiots, play!" shouted the proprietor, waving his arms excitedly.

Play they did.

Little Dimples, too, had by this time forgotten that she was resting, and now she began to ride as she never had ridden before, throwing a series of difficult backward turns, landing each time with a sureness that she never had before accomplished.

Tweetle! Tweetle!

The act came to a quick ending. The time for the equestrian act had expired, and it must give way to the others that were to follow. But Phil, instead of dropping to the ground and walking to the paddock along the concourse, suddenly brought down his whip on the gray's flanks, much to that animal's surprise and apparent disgust.

Starting off at a quicker gallop, the gray swung into the concourse, heading for the paddock with disapproving ears laid back on her head, Phil standing as rigid as a statue with folded arms, far back over the animal's hips.

The people were standing up, waving their arms wildly. Many hurled their hats at the Circus Boy in their excitement, while others showered bags of peanuts over him as he raced by them.

Such a scene of excitement and enthusiasm never had been seen under that big top before. Phil did not move from his position until he reached the paddock. Arriving there he sat down, slid to the ground and collapsed in a heap.

Mr. Sparling came charging in, hat missing and hair standing straight up where he had run his fingers through it in his excitement.

He grabbed Phil in his arms and carried him into the dressing tent.

"You're not hurt, are you, my lad?" he cried.

"No; I'm just a silly little fool," smiled Phil a bit weakly. "How did I do?"

"It was splendid, splendid."

"Hurrah for Phil Forrest!" shouted the performers. Then boosting the lad to their shoulders, the painted clowns began marching about the dressing tent with him singing, "For He's a Jolly Good Fellow."

"All out for the leaping act," shouted the callboy, poking his grinning countenance through between the flaps. "Leapers and clowns all out on the jump!"

CHAPTER XVIII
DOING A DOUBLE SOMERSAULT

Cool, confident a troop of motley fools and clean-limbed performers filed out from the dressing tent, on past the bandstand and across the arena to the place where the springboard had been rigged, with a mat two feet thick a short distance beyond it.

With them proudly marched Teddy Tucker.

Mr. Sparling, in the meantime, was patting Phil on the back.

"I'm in a quandary, Phil," he said.

"What about?" smiled the lad, tugging away at his tights.

"I want you out front and yet it would be almost a crime to take a performer like you out of the ring. Tell me honestly, where would you prefer to be?"

"That's a difficult question to answer. There is a terrible fascination about the ring, and it's getting a stronger hold of me every day I am out."

"Yes; I understand that. It's so with all of them. I was that way myself at first."

"Were you ever in the ring?"

"I clowned it. But I wasn't much of a performer. Just did a few simple clown stunts and made faces at the audience. Then I got some money ahead and started out for myself. If I'd had you then I would have had a railroad show long before this season," smiled the showman.

"On the other hand," continued Phil, "I am anxious to learn the front of the house as well as the ring. I think, maybe, that I could spend part of my time in the office, if that is where you wish me. If you can spare me from the parade, I might put in that time to decided advantage doing things on the lot for you," mused Phil.

"Spare you from the parade? Well, I should say so. You are relieved from that already. Of course, any time you wish to go out, you have the privilege of doing so.

Sometimes it is a change, providing one is not obliged to go," smiled the showman.

"Most of the performers would be glad if they did not have to, though."

"No doubt of it. But let's see; you have how many acts now? There's the flying rings, the elephant act and now comes the bareback act--"

"Yes; three," nodded Phil.

"That's too many. You'll give out under all that, and now we're talking about doubling you out in front. I guess we will let the front of the house take care of itself for the present."

Phil looked rather disappointed.

"Of course, any time you wish you may come out, you know."

"Thank you; I shall be glad to do that. I can do a lot of little things to help you as soon as I learn how you run the show. I know something about that already," grinned the lad.

"If you wish, I will double somebody up on your flying rings act. What do you say?"

"It isn't necessary, Mr. Sparling. I can handle all three without any difficulty, only the bareback act comes pretty close to the grand entry. It doesn't give me much time to change my costume."

"That's right. Tell you what we'll do."

"Yes?"

"We'll set the bareback act forward one number, substituting the leaping for it. That will give you plenty of time to make a change, will it not?"

"Plenty," agreed Phil.

"How about the flying rings. They come sometime later, if I remember correctly."

"Yes; the third act after the riding, according to the new arrangement. No trouble about that."

"Very well; then I will notify the director and let him make the necessary changes. I want to go out now and see your young friend make an exhibition of himself."

"Teddy?"

"Yes. He's going on the leaping act for the first time, you know."

"That's so. I had forgotten all about it. I want to see that, too. I'll hurry and dress."

"And, Phil," said the showman in a more kindly voice, even, than he had used before.

"Yes, sir," answered the lad, glancing up quickly.

"You are going to be a great showman some of these days, both in the ring and out of it. Remember what I tell you."

"Thank you; I hope so. I am going to try to be at least a good one."

"You're that already. You've done a lot for the Sparling Combined as it is and I don't want you to think I do not appreciate it. Shake hands!"

Man and boy grasped each other's hand in a grip that meant more than words. Then Mr. Sparling turned abruptly and hurried out into the big top where the leaping act was in full cry.

Painted clowns were keeping the audience in a roar by their funny leaps from the springboard to the mat, while the supple acrobats were doing doubles and singles through the air, landing gracefully on the mat as a round off.

The showman's first inquiring look was in search of Teddy Tucker. He soon made the lad out. Teddy was made up as a fat boy with a low, narrow-brimmed hat perched jauntily on one side of his head. There was drollery in Teddy's every movement. His natural clownish movements were sufficient to excite the laughter of the spectators without any attempt on his part to be funny, while the lad kept up a constant flow of criticism of his companions in the act.

But they had grown to know Teddy better, by this time, and none took his taunts seriously.

"That boy can leap, after all," muttered Mr. Sparling. "I thought he would tumble around and make some fun for the audience, but I hadn't the least idea he could do a turn. Why, he's the funniest one in the bunch."

Teddy was doing funny twists in the air as he threw a somersault at that moment. In his enthusiasm he overshot the mat, and had there not been a performer handy to catch him, the lad might have been seriously hurt.

Mr. Sparling shook his head.

"Lucky if he doesn't break his neck! But that kind seldom do," the owner said out loud.

Now the helpers were bringing the elephants up. Two were placed in front of the springboard and over these a stream of gaudily attired clowns dived, doing a turn in the air as they passed. Teddy was among the number.

Three elephants were lined up, then a fourth and a fifth.

"I hope he isn't going to try that," growled Mr. Sparling, noting that the lad was waiting his turn to get up on the springboard. "Not many of them can get away with that number. I suppose I ought to go over and stop the boy. But I guess he won't try to jump them. He'll probably walk across their backs, the same as he has seen the other clowns do."

Teddy, however, had a different plan in mind. He had espied Mr. Sparling looking at him from across the tent, and he proposed to let the owner see what he really could do.

For a moment the lad poised at the top of the springboard, critically measuring the distance across the backs of the assembled elephants.

"Go on, go on!" commanded the director. "Do you think this show can wait on your motion all day? Jump, or get off the board!"

"Say, who's doing this you or I?" demanded Teddy in well-feigned indignation, and in a voice that was audible pretty much all over the tent.

This drew a loud laugh from the spectators, who were now in a frame of mind to laugh at anything the Fat Boy did.

"It doesn't look as if anyone were doing anything. Somebody will be in a minute, if I hear any more of your talk," snapped the director. "Are you going to jump, or are you going to get off the board?"

"Well," shouted Teddy, "confidentially now, mind you. Come over here. I want to talk to you. Confidentially, you know. I'm going to jump, if you'll stop asking questions long enough for me to get away."

Amid a roar of laughter from spectators, and broad grins on the part of the performers, Teddy took a running start and shot up into the air.

"He's turning too quick," snapped Mr. Sparling.

Teddy, however, evidently knew what he was about. Turning a beautiful somersault, he launched into a second one with the confidence of a veteran. All the circus people in the big top expected to see the lad break his neck. Instead, however, Tucker landed lightly and easily on his feet while the spectators shouted their approval. But instead of landing on the mat as he thought he was doing, Teddy was standing on the back of the last elephant in the line.

His double somersault had made him dizzy and the boy did not realize that he had not yet reached the mat on the ground. Bowing and smiling to the audience, the Fat Boy started to walk away.

Then Teddy fell off, landing in a heap on the hard ground. He rose, aching, but the onlookers on the boards took it all as a funny finish, and gleefully roared their appreciation.

CHAPTER XIX
MAROONED IN A FREIGHT CAR

Catch him! Catch him! Catch that man!"

The parade was just passing when Phil shouted out the words that attracted all eyes toward him. It was to a policeman that he appealed.

The lad had discovered a shock of red hair above the heads of the people, and was gradually working his way toward the owner of it, when all at once Red Larry discovered him.

Red pushed his way through the crowd and disappeared down an alleyway, the policeman to whom the boy had appealed making no effort to catch the man.

"What kind of a policeman are you, anyway?" cried Phil in disgust. "That fellow is a crook, and we have been on the lookout for him for the last four weeks."

"What's he done?"

"Done? Tried to poison one of the elephants, and a lot of other things."

"The kid's crazy or else he belongs to the circus," laughed a bystander.

Phil Forrest did not hear the speaker, however, for the boy had dashed through the crowd and bounded into the alley where he had caught a glimpse of a head of red hair a moment before.

But Larry was nowhere in sight. He had disappeared utterly.

"I was right," decided Phil, after going the length of the alley and back. "He's been following this show right along, and before he gets through he'll put us out of business if we don't look sharp."

Considerable damage already had been done. Horses and other animals fell ill, in some instances with every evidence of poisoning; guy ropes were cut, and the cars had been tampered with in the railroad yards.

All this was beginning to get on the nerves of the owner of the show, as well as on those of some of his people who knew about it. Things had come to a point where it was necessary to place more men on guard about the lot to protect the show's property.

At each stand of late efforts had been made to get the police to keep an eye open for one Red Larry, but police officials do not, as a rule, give very serious heed to the complaints of a circus, especially unless the entire department has been pretty well supplied with tickets. Mr. Sparling was a showman who did not give away many tickets unless there were some very good reason for so doing.

Phil, in the meantime, had been at work in an effort to satisfy his own belief that Larry was responsible for their numerous troubles. Yet up to this moment the lad had not caught sight of Red; and now he had lost the scoundrel through the laxity of a policeman.

There was no use "crying over spilled milk," as Phil told himself.

The lad spent the next hour in tramping over the town where the circus was to show that day. He sought everywhere for Red, but not a sign of the fellow was to be found.

As soon as the parade was over Phil hastened back to the lot to acquaint Mr. Sparling with what he suspected.

"Do you know," said Phil, "I believe that fellow and his companion are riding on one of our trains every night?"

"What?" exclaimed the showman.

"You'll find I'm right when the truth is known. Then there's something else. There have been a lot of complaints about sneak thieves in the towns we have visited since Red left us. You can't tell. There may be some connection between these robberies and his following the show. I'm going to get Larry before I get through with this chase."

"Be careful, Phil. He is a bad man. You know what to expect from him if he catches you again."

"I am not afraid. I'll take care of myself if I see him coming. The trouble is that Red doesn't go after a fellow that way."

Phil went on in his three acts as usual that afternoon, after having spent an hour at the front door taking tickets, to which task he had assigned himself soon after his talk with Mr. Sparling.

It was instructive; it gave the boy a chance to see the people and to get a new view of human nature. If there is one place in the world where all phases of human nature are to be found, that place is the front door of a circus.

The Circus Boys, by this time, had both fitted into their new acts as if they had been doing them for years--Phil doing the bareback riding and Teddy tumbling in the leaping act, both lads gaining the confidence and esteem more and more every day of their fellow performers and the owner of the show.

That night, after the performance was ended, Phil stood around for a time, watching the men at work pulling down the tent. He had another motive, too. He had thought that perchance he might see something of the man he was in search of, for no better time could be chosen to do damage to circus property than when the canvas was being struck.

Then everyone was too busy to pay any attention to anyone else. Teddy had gone on to pay his usual evening visit to the accommodation car and at the same time make miserable the existence of the worthy who presided over that particular car.

Phil waited until nearly twelve o'clock; then, deciding that it would be useless to remain there longer, turned his footsteps toward the railroad yards, for he was tired and wanted to get to bed as soon as possible.

He found the way readily, having been over to the car once during the morning while out looking for Red Larry. The night was very dark, however, and the yards, at the end from which he approached them, were enshrouded in deep shadows.

On down the tracks Phil could see the smoking torches where the men were at work running the heavy cages and canvas wagons up on the flat cars. Men were shouting and yelling, the usual accompaniment to this proceeding, while crowds of curious villagers were massed about the sides of the yard at that point, watching the operations.

"That's the way I used to sit up and watch the circus get out of town," mused Phil, grinning broadly, as he began hunting for the sleeper where his berth was.

All at once the lights seemed to disappear suddenly from before his eyes. Phil felt himself slowly settling to the ground. He tried to cry out, but could not utter a sound.

Then the lad understood that he was being grasped in a vise-like grip. That was the last he knew.

When Phil finally awakened he was still in deep, impenetrable darkness. The train was moving rapidly, but there seemed to the boy to be something strange and unusual in his surroundings. His berth felt hard and unnatural. For a time he lay still with closed eyes, trying to recall what had happened. There was a blank somewhere, but he could not find it.

"Funny! This doesn't seem like No. 11. If it is, we must be going over a pretty rough stretch of road."

He put out both hands cautiously and groped about him. Phil uttered an exclamation of surprise.

"Good gracious, I'm on the floor. I must have fallen out of bed."

Then he realized that this could not be the case, because there was a carpet on the floor of No. 11.

This was a hard, rough floor on which he was lying, and the air was close, very different from that in the well-kept sleeping car in which he traveled nightly from stand to stand.

In an effort to get to his feet the lad fell back heavily. His head was swimming dizzily, and how it did ache!

"I wonder what has happened?" Forrest thought out loud. "Maybe I was struck by a train. No; that couldn't be the case, or I should not be here. But where am I? I might be in one of the show cars, but I don't believe there is an empty car on the train."

As soon as Phil felt himself able to sit up he searched through his pockets until he found his box of matches, which he always carried now, as one could not tell at what minute they might be needed.

Striking a light, he glanced quickly about him; then the match went out.

"I'm in a freight car," he gasped. "But where, where?"

There was no answer to this puzzling question. Phil struggled to his feet, and, groping his way to the door, began tugging at it to get it open. The door refused to budge.

"Locked! It's locked on the outside! What shall I do? What shall I do?" he cried.

Phil sat down weak and dizzy. There was nothing, so far as he could see, that could be done to liberate himself from his imprisonment. Chancing to put his hand to his head, he discovered a lump there as large as a goose egg.

"I know--let me think--something--somebody must have hit me an awful crack. Now I remember--yes, I remember falling down in the yard there just as if something had struck me. Who could have done such a cruel thing?"

Phil thought and thought, but the more he thought about it the more perplexed did he become. All at once he started up, with a sudden realization that the train was slowing down. He could hear the air brakes grating and grinding and squealing against the car wheels below him, until finally the train came to a dead stop.

"Now is my chance to make somebody hear," Phil cried, springing up and groping for the door again.

He shouted at the top of his voice, then beat against the heavy door with fists and feet, but not a sign could he get that anyone heard him.

As a matter of fact, no one was near him at that moment. The long freight train had stopped at a water tank far out in the country, and the trainmen were at the extreme ends of the train.

In a few moments the train started with such a jerk that Forrest was thrown off his feet. He sprang up again, hoping that the train might be going past a station there, and that someone might hear him. Then he began rattling at and kicking the door again.

It was all to no purpose.

Finally, in utter exhaustion, the lad sank to the floor, soon falling into a deep sleep. How long he slept he did not know when at last he awakened.

"Why, the train has stopped," Forrest exclaimed, suddenly sitting up and rubbing his eyes. "Now I ought to make somebody hear me because it's daylight. I can see the light underneath the door. I'll try it again."

He did try it, hammering at the door and shouting at intervals during the long hours that followed. Once more he lighted matches and began examining his surroundings with more care. Phil discovered a trap door in the roof, but it was closed.

"If only there were a rope hanging down, I'd be up there in no time," he mused. I wonder if I couldn't climb up and hang to the braces. I might reach it in that way. I'm going to try it."

Deciding upon this, the Circus Boy, after no little effort, succeeded in climbing up to one of the side braces in the car. >From the plates long, narrow beams extended across the car, thus supporting the roof. Choosing two that led along near the trap, Phil, after a few moments' rest, gripped one firmly in each hand from the underside and began swinging himself along almost as if he were traveling on a series of traveling rings, but with infinitely more effort and discomfort.

His hands were aching frightfully, and he knew that he could hold on but a few seconds longer.

"I've got to make it," he gasped, breathing hard.

At last he had reached the goal. Phil released one hand and quickly extended it to the trap door frame.

There was not a single projection there to support him, nor to which he might cling. His hand slipped away, suddenly throwing his weight upon the hand grasping the roof timber. The strain was too much. Phil Forrest lost his grip and fell heavily to the floor.

But this time he did not rise. The lad lay still where he had fallen.

CHAPTER XX
THE BARNYARD CIRCUS

When next Phil opened his eyes he was lying on the grass on the shady side of a freight car with someone dashing water in his face, while two or three others stood around gazing at him curiously.

"Whe--where am I?" gasped the boy.

"I reckon you're lucky to be alive," laughed the man who had been soaking him from a pail of water. "Who be ye?"

"My name is Phil Forrest."

"How'd ye git in that car? Stealing a ride, eh? Reckon we'd better hand ye over to the town constable. It's again the law to steal rides on freight trains."

"I've not stolen a ride. It's no such thing," protested Phil indignantly.

"Ho, ho, that's a rich one! Paid yer fare, hey? Riding like a gentleman in a side-door Pullman. Good, ain't it, fellows?"

"Friends, I assure you I am not a tramp. Someone assaulted me and locked me in that car last night. I've got money in my pocket to prove that I am not a tramp."

The lad thrust his hands into his trousers' pockets, then a blank expression overspread his face. Reaching to his vest to see if his watch were there, he found that that, too, was missing.

"I've been robbed," he gasped. "That's what it was. Somebody robbed and threw me into this car last night. See, I've got a lump on my head as big as a man's fist."

"He sure has," agreed one of the men. "Somebody must a given him an awful clout with a club."

"What town is this, please?"

"Mexico, Missouri."

"Mexico?"

"Yes."

"How far is it from St. Joseph?"

"St. Joseph? Why, I reckon St. Joe is nigh onto a hundred and fifty miles from here."

Phil groaned.

"A hundred and fifty miles and not a cent in my pocket! What shall I do? Can I send a telegram? Where is the station?"

"Sunday. Station closed."

"Sunday? That's so."

Phil walked up and down between the tracks rather unsteadily, curiously observed by the villagers. They had heard his groans in the freight car on the siding as they passed, and had quickly liberated the lad.

"Do you think I could borrow enough money somewhere here to get me to St. Joseph? I would send it back by return mail."

The men laughed long and loud.

"What are you in such a hurry to get to St. Joe for?" demanded the spokesman of the party.

"Because I want to get back to the circus."

"Circus?" they exclaimed in chorus.

"Yes. I belong with the Sparling Combined Shows. I was on my way to my train, in the railroad yards, when I was knocked out and thrown into that car."

"You with a circus?" The men regarded him in a new light.

"Yes; why not?"

This caused them to laugh. Plainly they did not believe him. Nor did Phil care much whether they did or not.

"What time is it?" he asked.

"Church time."

He knew that, for he could hear the bells ringing off in the village to the east of them.

"I'll tell you what, sirs; I have got to have some breakfast. If any of you will be good enough to give me a meal I shall be glad to do whatever you may wish to pay for it. Then, if I cannot find the telegraph operator, I shall have to stay over until

I do."

"What do you want the telegraph man for?"

"I want to wire the show for some money to get back with. I've got to be there tomorrow, in time for the show. I must do it, if I have to run all the way."

The men were impressed by his story in spite of themselves; yet they were loath to believe that this slender lad, much the worse for wear, could belong to the organization he had named.

"What do you do in the show?"

"I perform on the flying rings, ride the elephant and ride bareback in the ring. What about it? Will one of you put me up?"

The villagers consulted for a moment; then the spokesman turned to Phil.

"I reckon, if you be a circus feller, you kin show us some tricks, eh?"

"Perform for you, you mean?"

"Yep."

"Well, I don't usually do anything like that on Sunday," answered the Circus Boy reflectively.

"Eat on Sunday, don't you?"

"When I get a chance," Phil grinned. "I guess your argument wins. I've got to eat and I have offered to earn my meal. What do you want me to do?"

"Kin you do a flip?"

Phil threw himself into a succession of cartwheels along the edge of the railroad tracks, ending in a backward somersault.

"And you ride a hoss without any saddle, standing up on his back--you do that, too?"

"Why, yes," laughed Phil, his face red from his exertion.

"Then, come along. Come on, fellers!"

Phil thought, of course, that he was being taken to the man's home just outside the village, where he would get his breakfast. He was considerably surprised, therefore, when the men passed the house that his acquaintance pointed out as belonging to himself, and took their way on toward a collection of farm buildings some distance further up the road.

"I wonder what they are going to do now?" marveled Phil. "This surely doesn't look much like breakfast coming my way, and I'm almost famished."

The leader of the party let down the bars of the farmyard, conducting his guests around behind a large hay barn, into an enclosed space, in the center of which stood a straw stack, the stack and yard being surrounded by barns and sheds.

"Where are you fellows taking me? Going to put me in the stable with the live stock?" questioned Phil, laughingly.

"You want some breakfast, eh?"

"Certainly I do, but I'm afraid I can't eat hay."

The men laughed uproariously at this bit of humor.

"Must be a clown," suggested one.

"No, I am not a clown. My little friend who performs with me, and comes from the same town I do, is one. I wish he were here. He would make you laugh until you couldn't stand without leaning against something."

"Here, Joe! Here, Joe!" their guide began calling in a loud voice, alternating with loud whistling.

Phil heard a rustling over behind the straw stack, and then out trotted a big, black draft horse, a heavy-footed, broad-backed Percheron, to his astonishment.

"My, that's a fine piece of horse flesh," glowed the lad. "We have several teams of those fellows for the heavy work with the show. Of course we don't use them in the ring. Is this what you brought me here to see?"

"Yep. Git up there."

"What do you mean?"

"Git up and show us fellers if you're a real circus man."

"You mean you want me to ride him?" said Phil.

"Sure thing."

"How?"

"Git on his back and do one of them bareback stunts you was telling us about," and the fellow winked covertly at his companions, as much as if to say, "we've got him going this time."

"What; here in this rough yard?"

"Yep."

Phil considered for a moment, stamping about on the straw-covered ground, then sizing up the horse critically.

"All right. Bring me a bridle and fasten a long enough rein to the bit so I can get hold of it standing up."

He was really going to do as they demanded. The men were surprised. They had not believed he could, and now, at any rate, he was going to make an effort to make good his boast.

A bridle was quickly fetched and slipped on the head of old Joe. In place of reins the farmer attached a rope to the bridle, Phil measuring on the back of the horse to show how long it should be cut.

The preparations all complete, Phil grasped the rein and vaulted to the high back of the animal, landing astride neatly. This brought an exclamation of approval from the audience.

"Now git up on your feet."

"Don't be in a hurry. I want to ride him around the stack a few times to get the hang of the ring," laughed Phil. "It's a good, safe place to fall, anyway. Do I get some breakfast after this exhibition?" he questioned.

"That depends. Go on."

"Gid-dap!" commanded Phil, patting the black on its powerful neck. Then they went trotting around the stack, the men backing off to get a better view of the exhibition.

On the second round Phil drew up before them.

"Got any chalk on the place?" he asked.

"Reckon there's some in the barn."

"Please fetch it."

They did not know what he wanted chalk for, but the owner of the place hurried to fetch it. In the meantime Phil was slowly removing his shoes, which he threw to one side of the yard. Bidding the men break up the chalk into powder, he smeared the bottoms of his stockings with the white powder, sprinkling a liberal supply on the back of the horse.

"Here, here! What you doing? I have to curry that critter down every morning," shouted the owner.

Phil grinned and clucked to the horse, whose motion he had caught in his brief ride about the stack, and once more disappeared around the pile. When he hove in sight again, the black was trotting briskly, with Phil Forrest standing erect, far back on the animal's hips, urging him along with sharp little cries, and dancing about as much at home as if he were on the solid ground.

The farmers looked on with wide-open mouths, too amazed to speak.

Phil uttered a shout, and set the black going about the stack faster and faster, throwing himself into all manner of artistic positions.

After the horse had gotten a little used to the strange work, Phil threw down the reins and rode without anything of the sort to give him any support.

Probably few farm barnyards had ever offered an attraction like it before.

"Come up here!" cried the lad, to the lighter of the men. "I'll give you a lesson."

The fellow protested, but his companions grabbed him and threw him to old Joe's back. Phil grabbed his pupil by the coat collar, jerking him to his feet and started old Joe going at a lively clip.

You should have heard those farmers howl, at the ludicrous sight of their companion sprawling all over the back of the black, with Phil, red-faced, struggling with all his might to keep the fellow on, and at the same time prevent himself taking a tumble!

At last the burden was too much for Phil, and his companion took an inglorious tumble, head first into the straw at the foot of the stack, while the farmers threw themselves down, rolling about and making a great din with their howls of merriment.

"There, I guess I have earned my breakfast," decided the lad, dropping off near the spot where he had cast his shoes.

"You bet you have, little pardner. You jest come over to the house and fill up on salt pork and sauerkraut. You kin stay all summer if you want to. Hungry?"

"So hungry that, if my collar were loose, it would be falling down over my feet," grinned the lad.

CHAPTER XXI
WHEN THE CRASH CAME

There was rejoicing on the part of his fellows, and relief in the heart of Mr. Sparling when, along toward noon next day, Phil Forrest came strolling on the circus lot at St. Joseph.

His friends, the farmers, had not only given him food and lodging, but had advanced him enough money for his fare through to join the show. His first duty was to get some money from Mr. Sparling and send it back to his benefactors.

This done, Phil repaired to the owner's tent where he knew Mr. Sparling was anxiously waiting to hear what had happened to him.

Phil went over the circumstances in detail, while Mr. Sparling listened gravely at first, then with rising color as his anger increased.

"It's Red Larry!" decided Mr. Sparling, with an emphasizing blow of his fist on the desk before him.

"After I thought the matter over that was what I decided--I mean that was the decision I came to."

"Right. Another season I'll have an officer with this show. That's the only way we can protect ourselves."

"Do all the big shows carry an officer?" asked Phil.

"Yes; they have a detective with them--not a tin badge detective, but a real one. Don't try to go out today. Get your dinner and rest up for the afternoon performance. I think you had better go to the train in my carriage tonight. I'm not going to take any more such chances with you."

"I'll look out for myself after this, Mr. Sparling," laughed Phil. "I think it was only two days ago that I said I wasn't afraid of Larry--that he couldn't get me. But he did."

That afternoon, as Phil related his experiences to the dressing tent, he included the barnyard circus, which set the performers in a roar.

Phil felt a little sore and stiff after his knockout and his long ride in the freight car; but, after taking half an hour of bending exercises in the paddock, he felt himself fit to go on with his ring and bareback acts.

Both his acts passed off successfully, as did the Grand Entry in which he rode old Emperor.

That night, after the performance, Phil hurried to the train, but kept a weather eye out that he might not be assaulted again. He found himself hungry, and, repairing to the accommodation car for a lunch, discovered Teddy stowing away food at a great rate.

"So you're here, are you?" laughed Phil.

"Yep; I live here most of the time," grinned Teddy. "They like to have me eat here. I'm a sort of nest egg, you know. It makes the others hungry to see me eat, and they file in in a perfect procession. How's your head?"

"Still a size too large," answered Phil, sinking down on a stool and ordering a sandwich.

As the lads ate and talked two or three other performers came in, whereupon the conversation became more general.

All at once there came a bang as a switching engine bumped into the rear of their car. Teddy about to pass a cup of steaming coffee to his lips, spilled most of it down his neck.

"Ouch!" he yelled, springing up, dancing about the floor, holding his clothes as far from his body as possible. "Here, you quit that!" he yelled, poking his head out of a window. "If you do that again I'll trim you with a pitcher of coffee and see how you like that."

Bang!

Once more the engine smashed into them, having failed to make the coupling the first time.

Teddy sat down heavily in the middle of the car, just as Little Dimples tripped in. In one hand he held a sandwich half consumed, while with the other he was still stretching his collar as far from his neck as it would go.

"Why, Teddy," exclaimed Dimples, "what are you doing on the floor?"

"Eating my lunch. Always eat it sitting on the floor, you know," growled the boy, at which there was a roar from the others.

"What are they trying to do out there?" questioned Phil.

"Going to shift us about on another track, I guess. I was nearly thrown down when I tried to get on the platform. I never saw a road where they were so rough. Did you?"

"Yes; I rode on one the other night that could beat this," grinned Phil.

A few minutes later the car got under motion, pushed by a switching engine, and began banging along merrily over switches, tearing through the yard at high speed.

"We seem to be in a hurry 'bout something," grunted Teddy. "Maybe they've hooked us on the wrong train, and we're bound for somewhere else."

"No, I don't think so," replied Phil. "You should be used to this sort of thing by this time."

"I don't care as long as the food holds out. It doesn't make any difference where they take us."

"What section does this car go out on tonight, steward?" questioned Phil.

"The last. Goes out with the sleepers."

"That explains it. They are shifting us around, making up the last section and to get us out of the way of section No. 2. I never can keep these trains straight in my mind, they change them so frequently. But it's better than riding in a canvas wagon over a rough country road, isn't it, Teddy?"

"Worse," grunted the lad. "You never know when you're going to get your everlasting bump, and you don't have any net to fall in when you do. Hey, they're at it again!"

His words were almost prophetic.

There followed a sudden jolt, a deafening crash, accompanied by cries from the cooks and waiters at the far end of the car.

"Get a net!" howled Teddy.

"We're off the rails," cried the performers.

"Look out for yourselves!"

Little Dimples was hurled from her stool at the lunch counter, and launched straight toward a window from which the glass was showering into the car.

Phil made a spring, catching her in his arms. But the impact and the jolt were too much for him. He went down in a heap, Little Dimples falling half over him.

He made a desperate grab for her, but the woman's skirts slipped through his hand and she plunged on toward the far end of the car.

"Look out for the coffee boiler."

A yell from a waiter told them that the warning had come too late. The man had gotten a large part of the contents of the boiler over him.

But all at once those in the car began to realize that something else was occurring. Somehow, they could feel the accommodation car wavering as if on the brink of a precipice. Then it began to settle slowly and the mystified performers and car hands thought it was going to rest where it was on the ties.

Instead, the car took a sudden lurch.

"We're going over something!" cried a voice.

Phil, who had scrambled quickly to his feet, half-dazed from the fall, stood irresolutely for a few seconds then began making his way toward where Little Dimples had fallen.

At that moment young Forrest was hurled with great force against the side of the car. Everything in the car seemed suddenly to have become the center of a miniature cyclone. Dishes, cooking utensils, tables and chairs were flying through the air, the noise within the car accompanied by a sickening, grinding series of crashes from without.

Groans were already distinguishable above the deafening crashes.

Those who were able to think realized that the accommodation car was falling over an embankment of some sort.

Through accident or design, what is known as a "blind switch" had been turned while the engine was shunting the accommodation car about the yards. The result was that the car had left the rails, bumped along on the ties for a distance, then had toppled over an embankment that was some twenty feet high.

It seemed as if all in that ill-fated car must be killed or maimed for life. A series of shrill blasts from the engine called for help.

The crash had been heard all over the railroad yards. Railroad men and circus men had rushed toward the spot where the accommodation car had gone over the embankment, Mr. Sparling among the number. He had just arrived at the yards

when the accident occurred.

Fortunately, the wrecking crew was ready for instant service, and these men were rushed without an instant's delay to the outskirts of the yard where the wreck had occurred.

However, ere the men got there a startling cry rose from hundreds of throats.

"Fire! The car is on fire!"

"Break in the doors! Smash the sides in!"

Yet no one seemed to have the presence of mind to do anything. Phil had been hurled through a broken widow, landing halfway down the bank, on the uphill side of the car, else he must have been crushed to death. But so thoroughly dazed was he that he was unable to move.

Finally someone discovered him and picked him up.

"Here's one of them," announced a bystander. "It's a kid, too."

Mr. Sparling came charging down the bank.

"Who is it? Where is he?" he bellowed.

"Here."

"It's Phil Forrest," cried one of the showmen, recognizing the lad, whose face was streaked where it had been cut by the jagged glass in the broken window.

"Is he killed?"

"No; he's alive. He's coming around now."

Phil sat up and rubbed his eyes.

All at once he understood what had happened. He staggered to his feet holding to a man standing beside him.

"Why don't you do something?" cried Phil. "Don't you know there are people in that car?"

"It's burning up. Nobody dares get in till the wreckers can get here and smash in the side of the car," was the answer.

"What?" fairly screamed Phil Forrest. "Nobody dares go in that car? Somebody does dare!"

"Come back, come back, Phil! You can't do anything," shouted a fellow performer.

But the lad did not even hear him. He was leaping, falling and rolling down the bank, regardless of the danger that he was approaching, for the flames already showed through a broken spot in the roof of the car, which was lying half on its side at the foot of the embankment.

Without an instant's hesitation Phil, as he came up alongside, raised a foot, smashing out the remaining pieces of glass in a window. Then he plunged in head first.

The spectators groaned.

"Dimples! Dimples!" he shouted. "Are you alive?"

"Yes, here. Be quick! I'm pinned down!"

Phil rushed to her assistance. Her legs were pinioned beneath a heavy timber. Phil attacked it desperately, tugging and grunting, the perspiration rolling down his face, for the heat in there was now almost more than he could bear.

With a mighty effort he wrenched the timber from the prostrate woman, then quickly gathered her up in his arms.

"I knew you'd come, Phil, if you were alive," she breathed, her head resting on his shoulder.

"Do you know where Teddy is?" he asked, plunging through the blinding smoke to the window where voices already were calling to him.

"At the other end--I think," she choked.

The lad passed her out to waiting arms.

"Come out! Come out of that!" bellowed the stentorian voice of Mr. Sparling. But Phil had turned back.

"Teddy!" he called, the words choked back into his throat by the suffocating smoke.

"Wow! Get me out of here. I'm--I'm," then the lad went off into a violent fit of coughing.

By this time two others, braver than the rest, had climbed in through the window.

"Where are they all?" called a voice.

"I don't know. You'll have to hunt for them. I'm after you, Teddy. Are you held down by something, too?"

"The whole car's on me, and I'm burning up."

Phil, guided by the boy's voice, groped his way along and soon found his hands gripped by those of his little companion.

"Where are you fast?"

"My feet!"

It proved an easy matter to liberate Teddy and drag him to the window, where Phil dumped him out.

Mr. Sparling had climbed in by this time, and the wrecking crew were thundering at the roof to let the smoke and flames out, while others had crawled in with their fire extinguishers.

There were now quite a number of brave men in the car all working with desperate haste to rescue the imprisoned circus people.

"All out!" bellowed the foreman of the wrecking crew. "The roof will be down in a minute!"

"All out!" roared Mr. Sparling, himself making a dash for a window.

Others piled out with a rush, the flames gaining very rapid headway now.

"Phil! Phil! Where's Forrest?" called Mr. Sparling.

"He isn't here. Maybe--"

"Then he's in that car. He'll be burned alive! No one can live five minutes in there now!"

The fire department had arrived on the scene, and the men were running two lines of hose over the tracks.

"Phil in there?"

It was a howl--a startled howl rather than a spoken question. The voice belonged to Teddy Tucker.

Teddy rushed through the crowd, pushing obstructors aside, and hurled himself through the window into the burning car. He looked more like a big, round ball than anything else.

No sooner had Tucker landed fairly inside than he uttered a yell.

"Phil!"

There was no answer.

"Where--"

Teddy went down like a flash, bowled over by a heavy stream of water from the firemen's hose.

As it chanced he fell prone across a heap of some sort, choking and growling with rage at what had befallen him.

"Phil!"

"Yes," answered a voice from the heap.

"I've got him!" howled Teddy, springing up and dragging the half-dazed Phil Forrest to the window. There both boys were hauled out, Teddy and Phil collapsing on the embankment from the smoke that they had inhaled.

"Phil! Teddy!" begged Mr. Sparling, throwing himself beside them.

"Get a net!" muttered Teddy, then swooned.

CHAPTER XXII
WHAT HAPPENED TO A PACEMAKER

Find out how that car came to tumble off," were the first words Phil uttered after they had restored him to consciousness.

Teddy, however, was bemoaning the loss of the sandwich that he had bought but had not eaten.

"The accident shall be investigated by me personally before this section leaves the yard," said Mr. Sparling. "I am glad you suggested it, Phil. How do you feel?"

"I am all right. Did somebody pull me out?"

"Yes, Teddy did. You are a pair of brave boys. I guess this outfit knows now the stuff you two are made of, if it never did before," glowed Mr. Sparling.

"How many were killed?"

"None. The head steward has a broken leg, one waiter a few ribs smashed in, and another has lost a finger. I reckon the railroad will have a nice bill of damages to pay for this night's work. Were you in the car when it occurred?"

"Yes. They had been handling it rather roughly. We spoke of it at the time. We were moving down the yard when suddenly one end seemed to drop right off the track as if we had come to the end of it."

Mr. Sparling nodded.

"I'll go into it with the railroad people at once. You two get into your berths. Can you walk?"

"Oh, yes."

"How about you, Tucker,"

"I can creep all right. I learned to do that when I was in long pants."

"I guess you mean long dresses," answered the showman.

"I guess I do."

The boys were helped to the sleeper, where they were put to bed. Phil had been slightly burned on one hand while Teddy got what he called "a free hair cut," meaning that his hair had been pretty well singed. Otherwise they were none the worse for their experiences, save for the slight cuts Phil had received by coming in contact with broken glass and some burns from the coffee boiler.

They were quite ready to go to sleep soon after being put to bed, neither awakening until they reached the next show town on the following morning.

When the two lads pulled themselves up in their berths the sun was well up, orders having been given not to disturb them.

"Almost seven o'clock, Teddy," cried Phil.

"Don't care if it's seventeen o'clock," growled Teddy. "Lemme sleep."

"All right, but you will miss your breakfast."

That word "breakfast" acted almost magically on Tucker. Instantly he landed in the middle of the aisle on all fours, and, straightening up, began groping sleepily for his clothes.

Phil laughed and chuckled.

"How do you feel, Teddy?"

"Like a roast pig being served on a platter in the cook tent. Do you need a net this morning?"

"No, I think not. I'm rather sore where I got cut, but I guess I am pretty fit otherwise."

After washing and dressing the lads set out across the fields for the lot, which they could see some distance to the west of the sidings, where their sleepers had been shifted. Both were hungry, for it is not an easy matter to spoil a boy's appetite. Railroad wrecks will not do it in every case, nor did they in this.

But, before the morning ended, the cook tent had seen more excitement than in many days--in fact more than at any time so far that season.

The moment Phil and Teddy strolled in, each bearing the marks of the wreck on face and head everybody, except the Legless Man, stood up. Three rousing cheers and a tiger for the Circus Boys, were given with a will, and then the lads found themselves the center of a throng of performers, roustabouts and freaks all of whom showered their congratulations on the boys for their heroism in saving other's lives at the risk of their own.

Little Dimples was not one whit behind the others. She praised them both, much to Phil's discomfiture and Teddy's pleasure.

"Teddy, you are a hero after all," she beamed.

"Me? Me a hero?" he questioned, pointing to himself.

"Yes, you. I always knew you would be if you had half a chance. Of course Phil had proved before that he was."

Teddy threw out his chest, thrusting both hands in his trousers pockets.

"Oh, I don't know. It wasn't so much. How'd you get out?"

"Your friend, Phil, here, is responsible for my not being in the freak class this morning. There's Mr. Sparling beckoning to you. I think he wants you both."

The boys walked over as soon as they could get away from the others. That morning they sat at the executive table with the owner of the show, his wife and the members of Mr. Sparling's staff.

For once Teddy went through a meal with great dignity, as befitted one who was in the hero class.

"What happened to cause the wreck last night?" asked Phil, turning to his host of the morning at the first opportunity.

"The car went off over a blind switch that had been opened."

"By whom?"

"Ah, that's the question."

"Perhaps one of the railroad men opened it by mistake," suggested Teddy. "Nobody else would have a key."

"You'll find no railroad man made that blunder," replied Phil.

"No! While the railroad is responsible for the damages, I hardly think they are for the wreck. No key was used to open the switch."

"No key?"

"No."

"How, then?"

"The lock was wrenched off with an iron bar and the switch wedged fast, so there could be no doubt about what would happen. It might have happened to some other car not belonging to us, though it was a pretty safe gamble that it would catch one of ours."

"I thought as much," nodded Phil. "But perhaps its just as well."

"What do you mean by that?" questioned the showman sharply.

"That the railroad folks will do what the police are too lazy to do."

"What?"

"Get after the fellow who did it," suggested Phil wisely.

"That's so! That's so! I hadn't thought of it in that light before. You've got a long head, my boy. You always have had, for that matter as long as I have known you, so it stands to reason that you must always have been that way."

Teddy, having finished his breakfast, excused himself and strolled off to another part of the tent where he might find more excitement. He sat down in his own place near the freak table and began talking shop with some of the performers, while Phil and Mr. Sparling continued their conversation.

"I haven't given up hopes of catching him myself, Mr. Sparling."

"You came pretty close to it Saturday night."

"And I wasn't so far from it last night either," laughed the boy. "Going to be able to save the accommodation car?"

"No, it's a hopeless wreck."

"You probably will not put on another this season then?"

"What would you suggest?"

"I should not think it would be advisable. Most of the people go downtown, anyway, to get their lunch after the show."

"Exactly. That's the way it appeared to me, but I wanted to get your point of view." It was not that the owner had not made up his mind, but that he wanted to get Phil Forrest's mind working from the point of view of the manager and owner of a circus, seeing in Phil, as he did, the making of a future great showman.

All at once their conversation was disturbed by a great uproar at the further end of the tent, near where Teddy sat.

Two midgets, arguing the question as to which of them was the Smallest Man in the World, had become so heated that they fell to pummeling each other with their tiny fists.

Instantly the tent was in confusion, and with one accord the performers and freaks gathered around to watch the miniature battle.

A waiter in his excitement, stepped in a woodchuck hole, spilling a bowl of steaming hot soup down the Fat Woman's neck.

"Help! Help! I'm on fire!" she shrieked.

Teddy, now that he had become a hero, felt called upon to hurry to the rescue. Seizing a pitcher of ice water, he leaped over a bench and dumped the contents of the pitcher over the head of the Fattest Woman on Earth. Several chunks of ice, along with a liberal quantity of the water, slid down her neck.

This was more than human flesh could stand. The Fat Woman staggered to her feet uttering a series of screams that might have been heard all over the lot, while those on the outside came rushing in to assist in what they believed to be a serious disturbance.

Mr. Sparling pushed his way through the crowd, roaring out command after command, but somehow, the ring about the Fat Woman and the fighting midgets did not give way readily. The show people were too much engrossed in the funny spectacle of the midgets to wish to be disturbed.

Not so Teddy Tucker.

Having quenched the fire that was consuming the Fat Woman, he pushed his way through the crowd, with the stern command, "Stand aside here!" and fell upon the Lilliputian gladiators.

"Break away!" roared Teddy, grasping each by the collar and giving him a violent tug.

What was his surprise when both the little men suddenly turned upon him and started pushing and beating him.

Taken unawares, Teddy began to back up, to the accompaniment of the jeers of the spectators.

The crowd howled its appreciation of the turn affairs had taken, Teddy steadily giving ground before the enraged Lilliputians.

As it chanced a washtub filled with pink lemonade that had been prepared for the thirsty crowds stood directly in the lad's path. If anyone observed it, he did not so inform Teddy.

All at once the Circus Boy sat down in the tub of pink lemonade with a loud splash, pink fluid spurting up in a veritable fountain over such parts of him as were not already in the tub.

Teddy howled for help, while the show people shrieked with delight, the lad in his efforts to get out of the tub, falling back each time, until finally rescued from his uncomfortable position by the owner of the show himself.

"That's what you get for meddling with other peoples' affairs," chided Phil, laughing immoderately as he observed the rueful countenance of his friend.

"If I hadn't meddled with you last night, you'd have been a dead one today," retorted the lad. "Anyway, I've made a loud splash this morning."

CHAPTER XXIII
SEARCHING THE TRAIN

Salt Lake City proved an unusual attraction to the Circus Boys, they having read so much of it in story and textbooks.

Here they visited the great Mormon Temple. During their two day stand they made a trip out to the Great Salt Lake where Teddy Tucker insisted in going in swimming. His surprise was great when he found that he could not swim at all in the thick, salty water.

The trip over the mountains, through the wonderful scenery of the Rockies and the deep canyons where the sunlight seldom reaches was one of unending interest to them.

Most of the show people had been over this same ground with other circuses many times before, for there are few corners of the civilized world that the seasoned showman has not visited at least once in his life.

It was all new to the Circus Boys, however, and in the long day trips over mountain and plain, they found themselves fully occupied with the new, entrancing scenes.

By this time both lads had become really finished performers in their various acts, and they had gone on through the greater part of the season without serious accident in their work. Of course they had had tumbles, as all showmen do, but somehow they managed to come off with whole skins.

For a time after the wreck of the accommodation car the show had no further trouble that could be laid at the door of Red Larry or his partner. However, after a few days, the reports of burglaries in towns where the show exhibited became even more numerous.

"We can't furnish police protection to the places we visit," answered Mr. Sparling, when spoken to about this. "But, if ever I get my hands on that red head, the fur will fly!"

Passing out of the state of Utah, a few stands were made in Nevada, but the jumps were now long and it was all the circus trains could do to get from stand to stand in time. As it was, they were not always able to give the parade, but the manager made up for this by getting up a free show out in front of the big top just before the afternoon and evening performances began.

Reno was the last town played in Nevada, and everyone breathed a sigh of relief as the tents were struck and the show moved across the line into California. The difficulty of getting water for man and beast had proved a most serious one. At Reno, however, a most serious thing had occurred, one that disturbed the owner of the show very greatly.

Many of the guy ropes holding the big top, had been cut while the performance was going on and most of the canvasmen and laborers were engaged in taking down and loading the menagerie outfit.

A wind storm was coming up, but fortunately it veered off before reaching Reno. The severed ropes were not discovered until after the show was over and the tent was being struck. Mr. Sparling had been quickly summoned. After a careful examination of the ropes he understood what had happened. Phil, too, had discovered one cut rope and the others, on his way from the dressing tent to the front, after finishing his performance.

But there was nothing now that required his looking up Mr. Sparling, in view of the fact that the canvas was already coming down. Yet after getting his usual night lunch in the town, the lad strolled over to the railroad yards intending to visit the manager as soon as the latter should have returned from the lot.

The two met just outside the owner's private car, a short time after the loading had been completed.

"Oh, I want to see you, Mr. Sparling, if you have the time."

"I've always time for that. I was in hopes I would get a chance to have a chat with you before we got started. Will you come in?"

"Yes, thank you."

Entering the private car Mr. Sparling took off his coat and threw himself into a chair in front of his roll-top desk.

"Phil, there's deviltry going on in this outfit again," he said fixing a stern eye on the little Circus Boy.

Phil nodded.

"You don't seem to be very much surprised."

"I'm not. I think I know what you mean."

"You do? What for instance?"

"The cutting of those ropes tonight," smiled Phil.

"You know that?"

The lad nodded again, but this time with more emphasis.

"Is there anything that goes on in this outfit that you do not know about?"

"Oh, I presume so. If I hadn't chanced to walk over a place where there should have been a guy rope I probably never should have discovered what had been done."

"I'll bet you would," answered the owner, gazing at the lad admiringly.

"It is fortunate for us that we did not have a wind storm during the evening."

"Fortunate for the audience, I should say. Nothing could have held the tent with those ropes gone. It showed that the cordage had been cut by someone very familiar with the canvas. Almost a breath of wind would have caused the whole big top to collapse, and then a lot of people might have been killed. Well, the season is almost at an end now. If we are lucky we shall soon be out of it."

"All the more reason for getting the fellow at once," nodded Phil.

"Why?"

"After a few days we shall be closing, and then we shall not get an opportunity."

"That's good logic. I agree with you. I shall be delighted to place these hands of mine right on that fiend's throat. But first, will you tell me how I am going to do it? Haven't we been trying to catch him ever since those two men were discharged? Both of them are in this thing."

"I think you will find that there is only one now. I believe Larry is working alone. I haven't any particular reason for thinking this; it just sort of seems to me to be so."

"Any suggestions, Phil? I'll confess that I am at my wits' end."

"Yes, I have been thinking of a plan lately."

"What is it?"

"Have the trains searched."

"What?"

"You will remember my saying, sometime ago, that I believed the fellow was still traveling with us and--"

"But how--where could he ride that he would not be sure of discovery?" protested Mr. Sparling.

"He has friends with the show, that's how," answered Phil convincingly.

"You amaze me."

"All the same, I believe you will find that to be the case."

"And you would suggest searching the trains?"

"Yes."

"When?"

"Now. No; I don't mean at this very minute. I should suggest that tomorrow morning, say at daybreak, you send men over this entire train. Don't let them miss a single corner where a man might hide."

"Yes; but this isn't the only train in the show."

"I know. At the first stop, or you might do it here before we start, wire ahead to your other train managers to do the same thing. Tell them who it is you suspect. You'll be able to catch the squadron before they get in, though I do not believe our man will be found anywhere on that train."

"Why not?"

"The squadron went out before the guy ropes were cut."

"Great head! Great head, Phil Forrest," glowed the manager. "You're a bigger man than I am any day in the week. Then, according to your reasoning, the fellow ought either to be on this section or the one just ahead of it?"

"Yes. But don't laugh at me if I don't happen to be right. It's just an idea I have gotten into my head."

"I most certainly shall not laugh, my boy. I am almost convinced that you are right. At least, the plan is well worth carrying out. I'll give the orders to the train managers before we start."

"I would suggest that you tell them not to give the orders to the men until ready to begin the search in the morning."

"Good! Fine!" glowed the showman.

"I'm going to turn out and help search this section myself," said Phil. "You know I have some interest in it, seeing that it is my plan," he smiled.

"Better keep out of it," advised Mr. Sparling. "You might fall off from the cars. You are not used to walking over the tops of them."

"Oh, yes I am. I have done it a number of times this season just to help me to steady my nerves. I can walk a swaying box car in a gale of wind and not get dizzy."

Mr. Sparling held up his hands protestingly.

"Don't tell me any more. I believe you. If you told me you could run the engine I'd believe you. If there be anything you don't know how to do, or at least know something about, I should be glad to know what that something is."

"May I send your messages?" asked the lad. "If you will write them now I'll take them over to the station. It must be nearly starting time."

"Yes; it is. No; I'll call one of the men."

Mr. Sparling threw up his desk and rapidly scribbled his directions to the train managers ahead. After that he sent forward for the manager of their particular section, to whom he confided Phil Forrest's plan, the lad taking part in the discussion that followed. The train manager laughed at the idea that anyone could steal a ride on his train persistently without being detected.

Mr. Sparling very emphatically told the manager that what he thought about it played no part in the matter at all. He was expected to make a thorough search of the train."

"His search won't amount to anything" thought Phil shrewdly. "I'll do the searching for this section and I'll find the fellow if he is on board. I hope I shall. I owe Red Larry something, and I'm anxious to pay the debt."

The train soon started, Phil bidding his employer good night, went forward to No. 1 which was the forward sleeper on the train, next to the box and flat cars. He peered into Teddy Tucker's berth, finding that lad sound asleep, after which he tumbled into his own bed.

But Phil was restless. He was so afraid that he would oversleep that he slept very little during the night.

At the first streak of dawn he tumbled quietly from his berth, and, putting on his clothes, stepped out to the front platform, where he took a long breath of the fresh morning air.

The train was climbing a long grade in the Sierra Nevadas and the car couplings were groaning under the weight put upon them.

Phil climbed to the top of the big stock car just ahead of him, and sat down on the brake wheel.

Far ahead he saw several men going over the cars.

"They have not only begun the search but they are almost through," muttered Phil. "As I thought, they are not half doing it. I guess I'll take a hand."

Phil stood up, caught his balance and began walking steadily over the top of the swaying car. At the other end of the car he opened the trap door which was used to push hay through for the animals, examining its interior carefully. There was no sign of a stranger inside, nor did he expect to find any there.

"He'll be in a place less likely to be looked into," muttered the lad starting on again and jumping down to a flat car just ahead.

CHAPTER XXIV
CONCLUSION

There's somebody climbing over the train," called one of the searchers to the train manager.

All hands turned, gazing off toward Phil. He swung his hands toward them, whereat they recognized the lad and went on about their work.

"Wonder they saw even me!" grumbled the lad, moving slowly along. It seemed almost impossible that one could hide on a train like that. Here and there men were sleeping under the wagons, and Phil made it his business to get a look into the face of each of them. Not a man did he find who bore the slightest resemblance to Red Larry or Bad Eye.

"It doesn't look very promising, I must say," he muttered, jumping lightly from one flat car to another.

Phil had searched faithfully until finally he reached a "flat" just behind that on which stood the great gilded band wagon. Now, under its covering of heavy canvas, none of its gaudy trimmings were to be seen.

Phil sat down on the low projection at the side of the flat car, eyeing the band wagon suspiciously.

Somehow he could not rid himself of the impression that that wagon would bear scrutiny.

"I'll bet they never looked into it. Last year when we were a road show, I remember how the men used to sleep in there and how Teddy got thrown out when he walked on somebody's face," and Phil laughed softly at the memory. "I'm going to climb up there."

To do this was not an easy matter, for the band wagon seemed to loom above him like a tent. The canvas stretched over it, extending clear down to the wheels, to which it was secured by ropes. The only way the Circus Boy could get up into the wagon seemed to be to crawl under the canvas at the bottom and gradually to work his way up.

"I'm going to try it," he decided all at once. "Of course they didn't look into it. Maybe they are afraid they will find someone. Well, here goes! If I fall off that will be the last of me, but I am not going to fall. I ought to be able to climb by this time if I'm ever going to."

Phil got up promptly, glanced toward the long train that was winding its way up the steep mountain, then stepped across the intervening space between the two cars. He wasted no time, but immediately lifted the canvas and peered along the side of the wagon.

He discovered that he would have to go to the forward end of it in order to reach the top, because the steps were at that end. There the canvas was drawn tighter, so the lad untied one of the ropes, leaving one corner of the covering flapping in the breeze.

Cautiously and quietly he began climbing up, the wagon swaying dizzily with the motion of the train, making it more and more difficult to cling to it as he got nearer the top. The air was close, and soon after the boy began going up, the sun beat down on the canvas cover suffocatingly.

Now he had reached the top. High seats intervened between him and the other end, so that he could not see far ahead of him. Phil dropped down into the wagon and began creeping toward the rear.

He stumbled over some properties that had been stowed in the wagon, making a great clatter. Instantly there was a commotion in the other end of the car.

Phil scrambled up quickly and crawled over the high seat ahead of him. As he did so he uttered an exclamation. The red head of Red Larry could be seen, his beady eyes peering over the back of a seat.

"I've got you this time, Red!" exulted Phil, clambering over the seat in such a hurry that he fell in a heap on the other side of it.

The lad seemed to have no sense that he was placing himself in grave peril. He had no fear in his makeup, and his every nerve was centered on capturing the desperate, revengeful man who had not only assaulted Phil, but who had caused so much damage to the Sparling Shows.

"Don't you dare come near me, you young cub!" threatened Red, as with rage-distorted face he suddenly whipped out a knife.

Phil picked up a club and started toward him. The club happened to be a tent stake. Red observed the action, and crouching low waited as the lad approached him.

"I'm going to get you, Red! I'm not afraid of your knife. You can't touch me with it because before you get the chance I'm going to slam you over the head with this tent stake," grinned Phil Forrest.

Red snarled and showed his teeth.

"Oh, you needn't think you can get away. The men are hunting for you further up the train. They'll be along here in a minute, and then I reckon you'll be tied up and dumped into the lion cage, though I don't think even a lion would eat such a mean hound as you are."

Suddenly the man straightened up. Now, he held something in his hand besides the knife. It was a stake.

Red drew back his arm, hurling the heavy stick straight at his young adversary's head. Phil, observing the movement let drive his own tent stake, but having to throw so hurriedly, his aim was poor. Red Larry's aim, on the other hand was better. Phil dodged like a flash.

Had he not done so the stake would have struck him squarely in the face. As it was the missile grazed the side of his head, causing the lad to fall in a heap.

Red Larry hesitated only for a second, then leaping to the high rear seat of the wagon drew his knife along the canvas above him, opening a great slit in it. Through the opening thus made he peered cautiously. What he saw evidently convinced him of the truth of what Phil had just said. Up toward the head of the train the searchers were at work, and from what Red had heard he realized they were looking for him.

Red did not delay a second. He scrambled out through the canvas just as Phil pulled himself to his feet. The lad could see the fellow's legs dangling through the canvas.

Phil uttered a yell, hurling himself wildly over the high-backed seats in an effort to catch and hold the legs ere Red could get out. But Larry heard him coming, and quickly clambered down the back of the wagon to the deck of the flat car.

Phil once more grabbed up his own tent stake as he stumbled back through the wagon.

"I've got you!" yelled the boy as he pulled himself up through the opening, observing Red standing hesitatingly on the flat car with a frightened look in his eyes.

"Hi! Hi!" cried Phil, turning and gesticulating wildly at the men further up the train "I've got him! Hurry! I--"

Something sang by his head and dropped quivering in the canvas beyond him. It was the discharged tentman's knife which he had aimed at Phil, his aim having been destroyed by a lurch of the car, thus saving the Circus Boy's life.

"Want to kill me, do you? I've got you now! The men are coming. Don't you dare move or I'll drop this stake on you. I can't miss you this time."

Red after one hesitating glance, faced the front and leaped from the train down the long, sloping cinder-covered bank.

Phil let drive his tent stake. It caught Red on the shoulder, bowling the rascal over like a nine pin.

Phil Forrest uttered a yell of exultation, suddenly dropping to the floor of the car at the imminent risk of his life.

The men were now piling over the cars in his direction. He did not know whether they had seen Red jump or not. Phil did not waste any time in idle speculation.

"Come on!" he shouted, springing to the edge of the car, keeping himself from falling by grasping a wheel of the wagon.

Then Phil Forrest did a daring thing. Crouching low, choosing his time unerringly, he jumped from the train. Fortunately for him, the cars were running slowly up the heavy grade. But, slowly as they were going, the lad turned several rapid handsprings after having struck the ground, coming to a stop halfway down the slope, somewhat dazed from the shock and sudden whirling about.

But he was on his feet in a twinkling, and running toward the spot where Red was painfully picking himself up. Phil slipped and stumbled as the cinders gave way beneath his feet but ran on with a grim determination not to let his man escape him this time.

Both were now weaponless, so far as the lad knew. Red had possessed a revolver, but in his sudden jump from the train he had lost it, and there was now no time to look for it.

When he saw Phil pursuing, Larry started on a run, but the lad, much more fleet of foot, rapidly overhauled him, despite the handicap that Phil had at the start.

"You may as well give up! I'm going to catch you, if I have to run all the way across the Sierra Nevada Range," shouted Phil.

Red halted suddenly. Phil thought he was going to wait for him, but the lad did not slacken his speed a bit because of that.

All at once, as Phil drew near, Red picked up a stone and hurled it at his pursuer. Phil saw it coming in time to "duck," and it was well he did so, for Larry's aim was good.

"He must have been a baseball pitcher at sometime," grinned the lad. However, the fellow continued to throw until Phil saw that he must do something to defend himself else he would surely be hit and perhaps put out of the race altogether.

"So that's your game is it?" shouted the boy. "I can play ball, too."

With that the lad coolly began hunting about for stones, of which he gathered up quite an armful, choosing those that were most nearly round. In the meantime Red had kept up his bombardment, Phil dodging the stones skillfully. Then he too, began to throw, gradually drawing nearer and nearer to his adversary.

A small stone caught Phil a glancing blow on the left shoulder causing him to drop his ammunition. He could scarcely repress a cry, for the blow hurt him terribly. He wondered if his shoulder had not been broken, but fortunately he had received only a severe bruise.

It served, however, to stir Phil to renewed activity. Grabbing all the stones he could gather in one sweep of his hands he started on a run toward Red Larry, letting one drive with every jump. They showered around the desperate man like a rain of hail.

All at once Larry uttered a yell of pain and anger. One of Phil's missiles had landed in the pit of the fellow's stomach. Larry doubled up like a jacknife, and, dropping suddenly, rolled rapidly toward the foot of the slope.

Phil, still clinging to his weapons, ran as fast as his slender legs would carry him in pursuit of his man.

"I hit him! I hit him!" he yelled.

In a moment he came up with Larry, but the lad prudently stopped a rod from his adversary to make sure that the fellow was not playing him a trick. One glance sufficed to tell Phil that the man had really been hit.

"I hope he isn't much hurt, but I'm not going to take any chances."

Phil jerked off his coat and began ripping it up, regardless of the fact that it was his best. With the strands thus secured, he approached his prisoner cautiously, then suddenly jumped on him.

Larry was not able to give more than momentary resistance. Inside of three minutes Phil had the fellow's hands tied securely behind his back. Gathering the stones about him in case of need, the lad sat down and wiped the perspiration from his brow.

"I guess that about puts an end to your tricks, my fine fellow," announced Phil.

The train had been finally stopped, and a force of men now dashed back along the tracks. They had been in time to view the last half of the battle of the stones, and when Red went down they set up a loud triumphant yell. In a few minutes they had reached the scene and had taken the prisoner in tow.

The train was at the top of the grade waiting, so the show people and their captive were obliged to walk fully a mile to reach it. Mr. Sparling, attracted by the uproar, had rushed from his private car. He now met the party a little way down the tracks.

"I got him!" cried Phil, when he saw the owner approaching.

Red was carried to the next stop on the circus train. He was not much hurt and had fully recovered before noon of that day, much to Phil's relief, for he felt very badly that he had been obliged to resort to stone throwing. The lad would have preferred to use his fists. But, as the result of the capture, Red Larry was put where he would bother circus trains no more for some years. He was sentenced to a long term in prison.

The Great Sparling Shows moved on, playing in a few more towns, and, one beautiful morning drew up at the city by the Golden Gate. There the circus remained for a week, when the show closed for the season. But the lads were a long way from home, toward which they now looked longingly.

Mr. Sparling invited them to return with him in his private car which was to cross the continent attached to regular passenger trains, the show proper following at its leisure.

This invitation both boys accepted gladly, and during the trip there were many long discussions between the three as to the future of the Circus Boys. They had worked hard during the season and had won new laurels on the tanbark. But they had not yet reached the pinnacle of their success in the canvas-covered arena, though each had saved, as the result of his season's work, nearly twelve hundred dollars.

Phil and Teddy will be heard from again in a following volume entitled: "THE CIRCUS BOYS IN DIXIE LAND; Or, Winning the Plaudits of the Sunny South." Here they are destined to meet with some of the pleasantest as well as the most thrilling experiences of their circus career, in which both have many opportunities to show their grit and resourcefulness.

The Codes Of Hammurabi And Moses
W. W. Davies

QTY

The discovery of the Hammurabi Code is one of the greatest achievements of archaeology, and is of paramount interest, not only to the student of the Bible, but also to all those interested in ancient history...

Religion   **ISBN:** *1-59462-338-4*   **Pages:132**
MSRP $12.95

The Theory of Moral Sentiments
Adam Smith

QTY

This work from 1749. contains original theories of conscience amd moral judgment and it is the foundation for systemof morals.

Philosophy ISBN: *1-59462-777-0*   **Pages:536**
MSRP $19.95

Jessica's First Prayer
Hesba Stretton

QTY

In a screened and secluded corner of one of the many railway-bridges which span the streets of London there could be seen a few years ago, from five o'clock every morning until half past eight, a tidily set-out coffee-stall, consisting of a trestle and board, upon which stood two large tin cans, with a small fire of charcoal burning under each so as to keep the coffee boiling during the early hours of the morning when the work-people were thronging into the city on their way to their daily toil...

Childrens   ISBN: *1-59462-373-2*

Pages:84
MSRP $9.95

My Life and Work
Henry Ford

QTY

Henry Ford revolutionized the world with his implementation of mass production for the Model T automobile. Gain valuable business insight into his life and work with his own auto-biography... "We have only started on our development of our country we have not as yet, with all our talk of wonderful progress, done more than scratch the surface. The progress has been wonderful enough but..."

Biographies/   ISBN: *1-59462-198-5*

Pages:300
MSRP $21.95

www.bookjungle.com *email: sales@bookjungle.com fax: 630-214-0564 mail: Book Jungle PO Box 2226 Champaign, IL 61825*

The Art of Cross-Examination
Francis Wellman

QTY

I presume it is the experience of every author, after his first book is published upon an important subject, to be almost overwhelmed with a wealth of ideas and illustrations which could readily have been included in his book, and which to his own mind, at least, seem to make a second edition inevitable. Such certainly was the case with me; and when the first edition had reached its sixth impression in five months, I rejoiced to learn that it seemed to my publishers that the book had met with a sufficiently favorable reception to justify a second and considerably enlarged edition. ..

Pages:412

Reference   ISBN: *1-59462-647-2*   *MSRP $19.95*

On the Duty of Civil Disobedience
Henry David Thoreau

QTY

Thoreau wrote his famous essay, On the Duty of Civil Disobedience, as a protest against an unjust but popular war and the immoral but popular institution of slave-owning. He did more than write—he declined to pay his taxes,   and was hauled off to gaol in consequence. Who can say how much this refusal of his hastened the end of the war and of slavery ?

Law   ISBN: *1-59462-747-9*   **Pages:48**

MSRP $7.45

Dream Psychology Psychoanalysis for Beginners
Sigmund Freud

QTY

Sigmund Freud, born Sigismund Schlomo Freud (May 6, 1856 - September 23, 1939), was a Jewish-Austrian neurologist and psychiatrist who co-founded the psychoanalytic school of psychology. Freud is best known for his theories of the unconscious mind, especially involving the mechanism of repression; his redefinition of sexual desire as mobile and directed towards a wide variety of objects; and his therapeutic techniques, especially his understanding of transference in the therapeutic relationship and the presumed value of dreams as sources of insight into unconscious desires.

Pages:196

Psychology   ISBN: *1-59462-905-6*   *MSRP $15.45*

The Miracle of Right Thought
Orison Swett Marden

QTY

Believe with all of your heart that you will do what you were made to do. When the mind has once formed the habit of holding cheerful, happy, prosperous pictures, it will not be easy to form the opposite habit. It does not matter how improbable or how far away this realization may see, or how dark the prospects may be, if we visualize them as best we can, as vividly as possible, hold tenaciously to them and vigorously struggle to attain them, they will gradually become actualized, realized in the life. But a desire, a longing without endeavor, a yearning abandoned or held indifferently will vanish without realization.

Pages:360

Self Help   ISBN: *1-59462-644-8*   *MSRP $25.45*

www.bookjungle.com *email: sales@bookjungle.com fax: 630-214-0564 mail: Book Jungle PO Box 2226 Champaign, IL 61825*

QTY

The Rosicrucian Cosmo-Conception Mystic Christianity *by Max Heindel* ISBN: *1-59462-188-8* **$38.95**
The Rosicrucian Cosmo-conception is not dogmatic, neither does it appeal to any other authority than the reason of the student. It is: not controversial, but is: sent forth in the, hope that it may help to clear... New Age/Religion Pages 646

Abandonment To Divine Providence *by Jean-Pierre de Caussade* ISBN: *1-59462-228-0* **$25.95**
"The Rev. Jean Pierre de Caussade was one of the most remarkable spiritual writers of the Society of Jesus in France in the 18th Century. His death took place at Toulouse in 1751. His works have gone through many editions and have been republished... Inspirational/Religion Pages 400

Mental Chemistry *by Charles Haanel* ISBN: *1-59462-192-6* **$23.95**
Mental Chemistry allows the change of material conditions by combining and appropriately utilizing the power of the mind. Much like applied chemistry creates something new and unique out of careful combinations of chemicals the mastery of mental chemistry... New Age Pages 354

The Letters of Robert Browning and Elizabeth Barret Barrett 1845-1846 vol II ISBN: *1-59462-193-4* **$35.95**
by Robert Browning and Elizabeth Barrett Biographies Pages 596

Gleanings In Genesis (volume I) *by Arthur W. Pink* ISBN: *1-59462-130-6* **$27.45**
Appropriately has Genesis been termed "the seed plot of the Bible" for in it we have, in germ form, almost all of the great doctrines which are afterwards fully developed in the books of Scripture which follow... Religion/Inspirational Pages 420

The Master Key *by L. W. de Laurence* ISBN: *1-59462-001-6* **$30.95**
In no branch of human knowledge has there been a more lively increase of the spirit of research during the past few years than in the study of Psychology, Concentration and Mental Discipline. The requests for authentic lessons in Thought Control, Mental Discipline and... New Age/Business Pages 422

The Lesser Key Of Solomon Goetia *by L. W. de Laurence* ISBN: *1-59462-092-X* **$9.95**
This translation of the first book of the "Lernegton" which is now for the first time made accessible to students of Talismanic Magic was done, after careful collation and edition, from numerous Ancient Manuscripts in Hebrew, Latin, and French... New Age/Occult Pages 92

Rubaiyat Of Omar Khayyam *by Edward Fitzgerald* ISBN: *1-59462-332-5* **$13.95**
Edward Fitzgerald, whom the world has already learned, in spite of his own efforts to remain within the shadow of anonymity, to look upon as one of the rarest poets of the century, was born at Bredfield, in Suffolk, on the 31st of March, 1809. He was the third son of John Purcell... Music Pages 172

Ancient Law *by Henry Maine* ISBN: *1-59462-128-4* **$29.95**
The chief object of the following pages is to indicate some of the earliest ideas of mankind, as they are reflected in Ancient Law, and to point out the relation of those ideas to modern thought. Religiom/History Pages 452

Far-Away Stories *by William J. Locke* ISBN: *1-59462-129-2* **$19.45**
"Good wine needs no bush, but a collection of mixed vintages does. And this book is just such a collection. Some of the stories I do not want to remain buried for ever in the museum files of dead magazine-numbers an author's not unpardonable vanity..." Fiction Pages 272

Life of David Crockett *by David Crockett* ISBN: *1-59462-250-7* **$27.45**
"Colonel David Crockett was one of the most remarkable men of the times in which he lived. Born in humble life, but gifted with a strong will, an indomitable courage, and unremitting perseverance... Biographies/New Age Pages 424

Lip-Reading *by Edward Nitchie* ISBN: *1-59462-206-X* **$25.95**
Edward B. Nitchie, founder of the New York School for the Hard of Hearing, now the Nitchie School of Lip-Reading, Inc, wrote "LIP-READING Principles and Practice". The development and perfecting of this meritorious work on lip-reading was an undertaking... How-to Pages 400

A Handbook of Suggestive Therapeutics, Applied Hypnotism, Psychic Science ISBN: *1-59462-214-0* **$24.95**
by Henry Munro Health/New Age/Health/Self-help Pages 376

A Doll's House: and Two Other Plays *by Henrik Ibsen* ISBN: *1-59462-112-8* **$19.95**
Henrik Ibsen created this classic when in revolutionary 1848 Rome. Introducing some striking concepts in playwriting for the realist genre, this play has been studied the world over. Fiction/Classics/Plays 308

The Light of Asia *by sir Edwin Arnold* ISBN: *1-59462-204-3* **$13.95**
In this poetic masterpiece, Edwin Arnold describes the life and teachings of Buddha. The man who was to become known as Buddha to the world was born as Prince Gautama of India but he rejected the worldly riches and abandoned the reigns of power when... Religion/History/Biographies Pages 170

The Complete Works of Guy de Maupassant *by Guy de Maupassant* ISBN: *1-59462-157-8* **$16.95**
"For days and days, nights and nights, I had dreamed of that first kiss which was to consecrate our engagement, and I knew not on what spot I should put my lips..." Fiction/Classics Pages 240

The Art of Cross-Examination *by Francis L. Wellman* ISBN: *1-59462-309-0* **$26.95**
Written by a renowned trial lawyer, Wellman imparts his experience and uses case studies to explain how to use psychology to extract desired information through questioning. How-to/Science/Reference Pages 408

Answered or Unanswered? *by Louisa Vaughan* ISBN: *1-59462-248-5* **$10.95**
Miracles of Faith in China Religion Pages 112

The Edinburgh Lectures on Mental Science (1909) *by Thomas* ISBN: *1-59462-008-3* **$11.95**
This book contains the substance of a course of lectures recently given by the writer in the Queen Street Hall, Edinburgh. Its purpose is to indicate the Natural Principles governing the relation between Mental Action and Material Conditions... New Age/Psychology Pages 148

Ayesha *by H. Rider Haggard* ISBN: *1-59462-301-5* **$24.95**
Verily and indeed it is the unexpected that happens! Probably if there was one person upon the earth from whom the Editor of this, and of a certain previous history, did not expect to hear again... Classics Pages 380

Ayala's Angel *by Anthony Trollope* ISBN: *1-59462-352-X* **$29.95**
The two girls were both pretty, but Lucy who was twenty-one who supposed to be simple and comparatively unattractive, whereas Ayala was credited, as her Bombwhat romantic name might show, with poetic charm and a taste for romance. Ayala when her father died was nineteen... Ficiton/Classics Pages 484

The American Commonwealth *by James Bryce* ISBN: *1-59462-286-8* **$34.45**
An interpretation of American democratic political theory. It examines political mechanics and society from the perspective of Scotsman James Bryce Politics Pages 572

Stories of the Pilgrims *by Margaret P. Pumphrey* ISBN: *1-59462-116-0* **$17.95**
This book explores pilgrims religious oppression in England as well as their escape to Holland and eventual crossing to America on the Mayflower, and their early days in New England... History Pages 268

www.bookjungle.com *email: sales@bookjungle.com fax: 630-214-0564 mail: Book Jungle PO Box 2226 Champaign, IL 61825*

QTY

The Fasting Cure *by Sinclair Upton* ISBN: *1-59462-222-1* **$13.95**
*In the Cosmopolitan Magazine for May, 1910, and in the Contemporary Review (London) for April, 1910, I published an article dealing with my experi-
ences in fasting. I have written a great many magazine articles, but never one which attracted so much attention... New Age/Self Help/Health Pages 164*

Hebrew Astrology *by Sepharial* ISBN: *1-59462-308-2* **$13.45**
*In these days of advanced thinking it is a matter of common observation that we have left many of the old landmarks behind and that we are now pressing
forward to greater heights and to a wider horizon than that which represented the mind-content of our progenitors... Astrology Pages 144*

Thought Vibration or The Law of Attraction in the Thought World ISBN: *1-59462-127-6* **$12.95**
by William Walker Atkinson *Psychology/Religion Pages 144*

Optimism *by Helen Keller* ISBN: *1-59462-108-X* **$15.95**
*Helen Keller was blind, deaf, and mute since 19 months old, yet famously learned how to overcome these handicaps, communicate with the world, and
spread her lectures promoting optimism. An inspiring read for everyone... Biographies/Inspirational Pages 84*

Sara Crewe *by Frances Burnett* ISBN: *1-59462-360-0* **$9.45**
*In the first place, Miss Minchin lived in London. Her home was a large, dull, tall one, in a large, dull square, where all the houses were alike, and all the
sparrows were alike, and where all the door-knockers made the same heavy sound... Childrens/Classic Pages 88*

The Autobiography of Benjamin Franklin *by Benjamin Franklin* ISBN: *1-59462-135-7* **$24.95**
*The Autobiography of Benjamin Franklin has probably been more extensively read than any other American historical work, and no other book of its kind
has had such ups and downs of fortune. Franklin lived for many years in England, where he was agent... Biographies/History Pages 332*

Name	
Email	
Telephone	
Address	
City, State ZIP	

☐ **Credit Card**   ☐ **Check / Money Order**

Credit Card Number	
Expiration Date	
Signature	

Please Mail to: *Book Jungle*
PO Box 2226
Champaign, IL 61825
or Fax to: *630-214-0564*

ORDERING INFORMATION

web*: www.bookjungle.com*
email*: sales@bookjungle.com*
fax*: 630-214-0564*
mail*: Book Jungle PO Box 2226 Champaign, IL 61825*
or PayPal *to sales@bookjungle.com*

Please contact us for bulk discounts

DIRECT-ORDER TERMS

**20% Discount if You Order
Two or More Books**
Free Domestic Shipping!
Accepted: Master Card, Visa,
Discover, American Express

www.ingramcontent.com/pod-product-compliance
Lightning Source LLC
Chambersburg PA
CBHW080822020726
47501CB00009B/2387